Coffee, Cream and Curry

The hawk stood there, silent, watching her. A snake coiled in her stomach.

Then Mr. Henley's mood changed. A smile crept across his lips and he spoke gently. "I know what the problem is. You're nervous. Don't worry about it, Beth. Nobody has to know. Let's just have our own little fun."

He cocked his head to one side as he watched her. The snake wound itself tighter. "You make me feel good and I make you feel good. You know I have money, and that's all you need, isn't it?" The voice was sickly sweet syrup – taunting, repulsing. "You could get anything you want. I'd make sure of it. Just share some pleasure with me and we'll both be happy. So…what about it?"

As he spoke he moved closer…and closer still. The snake coiled tight, tight in her belly, twisting her insides till she almost buckled over in pain. The man lifted his hand to touch her and she spun around, teeth bared, the knife pointing straight at his chest.

"If you touch me I sink this knife right in you belly." She spoke through clenched teeth, fighting to keep the snake inside. Her chest heaved with the rising urge to strike. "I prepare to go to prison before I let you put your nasty hands on me."

Coffee, Cream and Curry

JUDY POWELL

Treasure Isle
BOOKS

TREASURE ISLE BOOKS
Published by:
Lyons Publishing Limited
4080 Living Arts Drive
Suite 402
Mississauga, Ontario, L5B 4N3
Canada
www.lyonspublishing.com

Canadian Cataloguing in Publication Data

Powell, Judy –

Coffee, Cream and Curry – 1st ed.

ISBN 978-0-9738590-1-0

1. Jamaica History Fiction. I. Title.

Cover design by: www.mariondesigns.com
Book Layout by: Lisa Gibson – www.renmanserv.com
Edited by: Beth Anderson

Printed in Canada

Dedicated to the memory of my dear mother and friend,
Evelyn May Powell

Her love of the English Language fostered the same in me. I will always be grateful for her example, her love and her guidance.

Mama, this book is for you.

ACKNOWLEDGEMENTS

Byron "Bobby" Treasure, it all began with this story, and it all began with you. I will always be grateful to you for giving me the 'kick in the seat of the pants' that I needed to get my writing career going. Thank you for believing in me, and for giving me the confidence to get my work out and into the hands of readers around the world.

Hotclue, what can I say? You have been there for me, unselfishly sharing your expertise and giving advice. You are such a great source of inspiration.

To friends and family who gave me words of encouragement, thank you all so much. Your words were the fuel that kept my light burning.

Thank you all!

Prologue

At the time of her birth the island had been gentle and kind, populated by a nation of peace-loving people who knew little of wars and violence. They were simple fisher-folk who spent their days raising gentle-spirited children with flattened foreheads. Every day the small-bodied men would take their narrow canoes out to sea while the boys snared wild birds and the women cleared the land and planted sweet potatoes and maize. In the evenings they would gather together to eat roasted fish and cassava cakes.

The women were well-practiced in the proper preparation of their staple food, cassava, which was poisonous in its natural state and required great care before the flour into which it was pounded could be formed into flat cakes and baked. They were experts in communal living. Everyone shared in the work to provide for the tribe's needs and at the end of the day they retired to large thatch houses, each of which was shared by several families. Under the leadership of the Cacique the people fished and farmed by day, and relaxed and smoked tobacco by night.

Although the island had been home to these Indians for over one hundred years imperial documents would state that the official year of her birth was 1494, the year Christopher Columbus landed on her northern shores.

He had been told that she was rich in gold but her riches lay in her lush, green beauty and her peaceful nature. In the east the invaders found rolling green hills and a mountain reaching into the clouds. In the west were open plains bordered by white sand and a translucent blue sea. The visitors were unimpressed by the island's serenity and beauty. Instead of embracing her children they raped and tortured them, infected them with diseases, and attacked them with dogs – for sport.

Within eighty years of the Spaniards' discovery of Xaymaca all her gentle inhabitants were dead. The brown-skinned Arawaks made way for white Spaniards and black Africans. The black slaves were rebellious. Some ran off and sought refuge in the island's bosom where they established their own settlements. They were called Maroons from the Spanish name for them, "cimmarron" – wild.

By 1655 the poorly protected island was captured by the British and became a jewel in the English crown. More slaves were brought in from Africa, sugar plantations flourished, and tobacco and rum were in good supply. The island's nature changed over the years from peaceful to violent, to wicked. She became the harlot of the Caribbean. With the British came the buccaneers who settled in the small sea town of Port Royal. They drank rum, ate smoked wild pig, and pirated Spanish ships. Within a decade and a half of the arrival of the British, Port Royal was known as the wealthiest and wickedest city in the world. Henry Morgan, the greatest pirate and buccaneer captain, was appointed Lieutenant Governor of the island in 1673. Port Royal's wickedness was finally swallowed up by the sea when most of the town was destroyed by earthquake in 1692.

Despite several slave rebellions the number of sugar plantations grew so that by 1739 the island housed almost four hundred and thirty of them. By 1807 when the trading of African slaves was abolished the island was teeming with black people. The slaves were emancipated in 1834 but continued to serve their masters under an apprenticeship system for four more years until slavery was finally abolished in 1838. For the next one hundred years the black people toiled on the land, surviving for the most part as small farmers. They were joined by the brown ones from India who came in from 1845 – 1917 as indentured labourers, then by the yellow ones from China and the pale-skinned Syrians who came in as traders and merchants.

Now over five centuries old, the island has seen peace and violence, bondage and freedom, struggle and triumph. She has been mother to the children of the world; their customs and creeds have blended to form a rich mélange of culture, music and cuisine.

This island, so rich in physical beauty, so complex in personality, is no child but a woman who smiles at the world through eyes misted with tears, seducing onlookers with promises of pleasure, paradise, no problem – hiding her diamond heart, so hardened by the tears of her offspring. This is Jamaica's story.

Chapter 1

1814

The boys' shouts rang out as they kicked the grapefruit around the dusty clearing. Chickens dashed away trying desperately to avoid the flying legs but the children were oblivious, shouting at the top of their lungs, totally immersed in the game. The sun beat down on their bare backs, black and glistening with sweat, but the scorching tropical heat seemed only to feed more energy to their active bodies.

Suddenly, the smallest of the group snatched the grapefruit and, with the lithe agility of a tiger, spun around with it on his toe and drove towards the makeshift goal. With a snap of his foot he sent it flying between the palm leaves.

The whoops and cheers from his team deafened the shouts of the white-haired woman who was just exiting a nearby shack. She leaned heavily on a wooden walking stick and with each step she took her ponderous body shook. Her massive skirts swayed in the dust and she almost seemed in danger of tripping over them. By the time she got close enough for them to notice her, the boys had their team mate high on their shoulders, laughing and shouting, enjoying the moment of celebration.

"Oonu be quiet now! Me tell you already." The woman's voice was much stronger, firmer than her stooped body bespoke. Hands on her hips, she scolded, "You know today be the Lord's day! I doan' waan hear no more noise out here, you hear me?"

A stocky boy turned to her and said, "Aw, Mammy, de game soon done. We soon come."

The old woman glared at him then turned, grumbling, and shuffled back into the hut.

Joseph sat silently in the shadows of the thick bushes, chewing on a stalk of sugar cane. As the sweet nectar ran down his chin he wiped it away with the back of his hand. He had been watching the boys for close to an hour, almost as captivated by the game as they were. He had been rooting for the underdogs and when that team won the taste of victory was just as sweet on his tongue. A slight smile softened his thin lips as he lay back into the soft bed of ferns and looked up at the patches of blue sky through the lush, green foliage, enjoying the cool breeze on his face.

When he heard the boys heading back to the huts he sat up again and watched his team, still laughing and hugging one another, while the losers brought up the rear, mumbling amongst themselves. This was the norm. Joseph knew that the boys would regroup next Sunday and there would be another game, another challenge, another chance for victory.

He had seen it often enough. He had been coming here for the past four weeks, watching the boys from the bushes, sharing their game from a distance. His Sunday afternoons had gone by slowly, drearily, until that afternoon when he had dared to go down to the slave village. He had set off for the rows of huts, partly out of curiosity but mostly out of sheer boredom.

It was hard being a lone white boy on a West Indian plantation. Outside of his parents his only companion was a sister who, as far as he could see, thought him nothing but a pest and therefore had little use for him. Of course, there were other white people on the plantation, but it would never do to get too friendly with the employees. He knew that would be his father's position on the matter so he never even bothered to try. Furthermore, the white plantation staff – an overseer, two foremen, a bookkeeper and a carpenter – were all far more advanced in years than he so he doubted that he would have much in common with any of them.

Hence, he set off for the nethermost end of the plantation, not in search of the companionship he lacked, but in a desperate attempt to break the monotony of his existence. He felt that if he had to open another work of Dickens, or the goodly Bible which his father never ceased to press upon him, he would go mad.

That first Sunday he had pretended exceeding interest in a history text and had retired to his room only to slip out once the rest of the family was otherwise occupied. He made his way stealthily through the trees to the Negro compound. He felt that here, at least, there would be some sort of life and, more importantly, boys his own age. His pleasure was great when he arrived to find the group hard at play. He remained in the shelter of the heavy foliage at the edge of the clearing, breathing in the strong green scents and drinking in the lively scene. The envy he felt surprised him.

Ever since then this had been his weekly entertainment. He looked forward to it but knew that he had to be very careful. His father must never find out that he spent his Sunday afternoons watching slave boys at play. At sixteen he was expected to become serious about his school work. He was to be heir to this great plantation and needed to spend more time with his books, his father told him repeatedly. As the boys walked away Joseph rose and stretched his lanky body then turned in the direction of the plantation house. It was almost time for dinner and he was tired of being scolded for lateness.

Seven minutes later he was sitting at the mahogany dining table, picking at the chicken on his plate. The table was laden with bowls full of food – steaming pepper pot soup, rice and red beans, boiled yellow yams, stewed carrots and fried plantains. The spicy aroma from the tray of fried chicken filled his nostrils.

Normally he would have wolfed down the mouth-watering fare but today he found himself strangely without appetite, not able to shake his low spirits. He wondered how long it would last. Back in England his spells of depression took days to dissipate but the vivid green of the Jamaican landscape, the cloudless blue of the sky and the brilliance of the sun usually had him back to his normal self in quick time. Somehow, today was different.

"Joseph! Are you listening?" Rachel Gordon's nasal voice brought him back sharply to the present. Her thin lips were pursed in annoyance.

"Yes… yes, Mother." He pushed his spectacles higher up his nose and blinked, turning his full attention to the thin woman who sat frowning at him. Her brown hair, with its strands of grey, was pulled to the back of her head in a severe bun which made her narrow face seem even bonier. Her long nose added to the skeletal image.

The only pretty part of her face was the eyes, light brown and fringed with thick, black lashes.

Joseph had always been told that he resembled his mother. He had inherited her narrow face and brown eyes. He was grateful that she had not passed on her nose to him. He knew that his father had not married his mother for her looks, or even out of love – he had overheard his Aunt Millie discussing it with her husband when they had visited four years ago. It was Rachel's inheritance of a prosperous plantation in the West Indies that had allowed her to pick from multiple suitors. She had chosen Adam Gordon, they said, because he was the handsomest of the lot.

"You have totally ignored me for the last few minutes," his mother complained. "Have you heard a word I've said?"

"He's been daydreaming again," Katherine broke in. "He always has his head in the clouds. That's why he almost got kicked out of school last term."

Joseph glared at his sister but said nothing. Katherine was in one of her troublesome moods and he knew better than to engage her in a quarrel. She was a master of words – he did not stand a chance against her. Besides, this was a subject he had no desire to discuss in any detail with his parents.

"What is this about?" Adam Gordon was frowning at him.

Before he could reply Katherine blurted out, "He got into a fight, father."

"Joseph, that is not like you." The bearded man stared across the table at him. "Explain yourself, my good man!"

Joseph's heart sank. His father was never so formal as when he was angry. Lately his falls from grace had been frequent even though he tried his utmost to remain in the favour of the man he admired so much. After his sixteenth birthday his father began to demand much more from him. He chided him often for not being more serious about life, for not getting more involved in the affairs of the plantation, for not being more mature. Now he would have to defend another demonstration of his immaturity.

Joseph looked down at his plate and spoke in a low voice. "I didn't want to fight. They were picking on me."

"I heard it was because he was defending the nigger slaves," Katherine smirked then yelped as he gave her a sharp kick. Joseph's face felt warm and he knew that his pale skin was flushed.

"Will you be quiet," he muttered as Katherine rubbed her leg, scowling.

"Joseph, we have gone through this before." Adam Gordon's voice was stern. "There is no need for you to always jump to the defence of the slaves. I have already explained to you how things work in this world."

"But I was not talking about slaves, father. The argument was about a free black man."

"What are you talking about, boy?"

"It's just that…well, the other boys were saying that even though he was not a slave he shouldn't be allowed to vote like a white man can."

"And what did you say?"

"I said…" Joseph sucked in his breath, then continued in a rush, "I said that he was a free man so he had every right to vote if he wanted to." He stared at his father's stern face and set his mouth in a defiant line.

"Be very careful about what you are out there defending. All this is yours," Adam waved his fork in the direction of the open window, "so don't be stupid and say anything to jeopardize that."

"But I was talking about a free man!"

"Joseph, this discussion is closed. We have enough trouble with those bloody missionaries sticking their noses into the plantation business. If it were up to them we would have an island full of Blacks running around free, tearing up the place. Put us out of business, that's what the damned lot of them are trying to do. Well, it won't happen, not in this lifetime." He paused for breath then glared at Joseph. "Don't let me get any more news that you are defending Negroes. Do you understand me, sir?"

Joseph knew when to yield. "Yes, sir," he sighed.

He knew that there was more to his father's anger than was being expressed. The planters in Jamaica had been complaining for years about the steady increase in the price of slaves. Ever since the bill was signed in 1808 for the abolition of the African Slave Trade the value of slaves had increased and the missionaries, particularly the Quakers, were the targets of blame and abuse. It seemed that all the problems on the plantation were being blamed on them – if the slaves were slow to the task, if they asked for time to mourn their dead, if they had any association with the free Blacks, the missionaries were blamed.

The planters even complained that one day slavery itself might meet its demise at the hands of the self-righteous missionaries. Then where would the country be, they moaned. As far as they were concerned Jamaica was not ready for the wholesale freedom of the slaves and would not be so for a very long time because the only thing holding her together was the planter class. Take us away, they said, and she would perish.

"Stupid boy," Katherine jeered under her breath so that only he could hear. He refused to take the bait and remained silent, waiting for the moment to pass, waiting for them to forget, as usual, that he existed.

"I got a letter from Peter this morning," Katherine announced brightly.

"Did you, now?" Mrs. Gordon's eyes twinkled with interest as she turned to her daughter. "And what, pray tell, is the latest news from the dear boy?"

"He wants me to come visit his family for two whole months. May I go?" She turned pleading eyes to their father. "Father, may I, please?"

"It seems you have your heart set on this young man." Adam smiled at her.

"You know I do."

"Well, Princess, you have my blessing."

"Thank you, Father." Katherine jumped up and threw her arms around his stout neck.

Joseph rolled his eyes. As usual, the main thing on his sister's mind was marriage. She was twenty-one years old, five years his senior, and eager to catch the perfect husband. She had met Peter while visiting a cousin in London. He was a book-keeper at a well-known London firm and soon after meeting him Katherine announced that he was the one for her. She was ready to be the perfect society wife. She often complained that life on a plantation was not for her. She loathed the heat, the insects and the Negro slaves.

With the family's money and her good looks Katherine could have had a husband by now. Her heart-shaped face was fringed with curls. She had their father's small, straight nose and hazel eyes but her rosebud mouth, constantly set in a cute pout, was all her own. Katherine had been courted by men of good breeding but she had always been vocal about her ideal mate – a man who would be understanding and lenient; in Joseph's opinion, a man who would let her "wear the breeches".

He wondered if her stance was because she had seen the way their father had cowed their mother over the years. Maybe she did not want to have the same experience as Mother. From what he had heard of Peter, Katherine would have no trouble taking charge. He stared at the two women as they discussed the virtues of Peter and his family. Getting bored, he stopped listening and as his mind moved back to that afternoon's game a slight smile softened his lips.

"There he goes, daydreaming again." Katherine's voice broke into his thoughts.

He stared blankly at her grinning face then down at his half-eaten meal. He could not stomach another bite. Turning to his father, he said, "May I be excused?" At his father's nod Joseph excused himself from the table and headed for the stairs.

In his room, far from the maddening chatter of his sister and the reprimands of his parents, he relaxed and found escape in his thoughts. He lay on the canopied four poster bed and looked out the window at the leaves of the mango tree trembling in the summer breeze. His thoughts grew sombre as he remembered the harsh words of the boys at boarding school and the loneliness he felt when they refused to speak to him. Still, he did not regret anything that he had said and simply made up his mind to survive as he had always done, alone.

He jumped up off the bed, picked up a bag of hard biscuits from the window sill and went over to the canary which sat on its perch, staring out at him through the bars of its cage. "Hey, Jack," he whispered to his friend as he fed him a biscuit. "We don't need them, do we?" The bird chirped and he smiled. "I knew you would see it my way."

Next Sunday Joseph was in his usual hiding place, watching the game. It was a cool afternoon. The sky was grey and the fresh smell of rain was in the air. As the leaves of the coconut palm swayed in the soft breeze he lay on his stomach in the soft bed of ferns. He bit into a guava and peered through the leaves. The slave boys played with wild abandon. They had earlier lamented that next morning they would have to be up before daybreak to toil in the fields until the blazing sun disappeared behind the hills. Sunday was the only day they had to enjoy themselves as the boys they were, so they put their all into it.

The game was only halfway through when Joseph decided to go; it was a slow game and he was getting restless. He gathered his legs under him and stood slowly, stretching to ease the cramps then headed back through the bushes. As he walked his thoughts went back, as it so often did, to school and England. He wished he did not have to go back there to the drone of the schoolmaster, the grey skies, the boiled mutton and turtle soup, and the strain of fitting in.

Suddenly, a sharp scream ripped into his thoughts. It had come from the other side of the bushes. He quickly ducked and crept on hands and knees into the bushes, closer to where he had heard the noise. He stopped when he heard the sound of a girl's sobs. He peered through the leaves and gasped as he saw Frederick Johnson, the carpenter, sprawled on top of a skinny, black girl.

"No, Massa Johnson."

The girl was struggling violently, tearing at the man's face with her fingernails and kicking her legs frantically. Her eyes were wide with fear and her breath came in gasps. "Massa Johnson! Don't do it, sah. Please!"

"Shut up, girl. You do whatever I want, you hear me?" The bulky man growled as he grabbed her wrists and pinned them above her head in one of his huge fists. "Who d'ye think's in charge here?"

"But Massa, I nevah…"

"I said shut up." He slapped her hard across the face. "Now spread them legs and let me in."

The girl let out a wail as the man dug his knees between her legs and forced them apart. Grabbing a handful of her skirt he dragged it up to her waist and began to rip at her drawers.

"No!" The girl's shriek was agonizing.

"Let her go," Joseph shouted from his hiding place.

"Huh? Who's there?" The big man's head whipped around but the rest of his body remained frozen, his hand still clutching the girl's knickers.

"I said, let her go!"

Frederick Johnson quickly got up off the girl, pulling up his breeches as he stood. His eyes widened as Joseph pushed through the bushes and stepped into the clearing. Then his heavy brows came together in a frown.

"Squire Joseph," he growled, "what are ye doin' here?"

"Leave the girl alone, Mr. Johnson. Go find yourself a grown woman."

The bigger man looked like he was about to say something then seemed to decide against it. His eyes shot daggers but he only snorted and brushed at the leaves on his shirt. Without a word he turned, pushed his way through the thick foliage and disappeared.

Joseph let out his breath in a whoosh then turned his attention to the dark-skinned girl who still crouched in the leaves and broken bushes, trembling and sobbing. The collar of her dress was ripped open to reveal a slim ebony shoulder. Her yellow head wrap, which had come loose in the struggle, hung from one ear and revealed thick, woolly plaits. Kneeling, Joseph put out a hand and touched her on the shoulder. She jumped.

"It's alright," he said gently, "he's gone."

Still trembling, the girl raised wet eyes to stare up at him. She drew in a shaking breath and whispered, "Thank you, Massa. You save me life."

Joseph did not answer but simply leaned over and pulled the torn dress back onto her shoulder. Looking embarrassed, she pushed her skirt back over her knees then began fumbling at the head wrap.

"Here, let me help you." Joseph picked the brown leaves from her hair then watched as she tied the bright cloth around her head. He stood up and stretched out his hand. She hesitated for a moment then placed a small hand in his. As soon as he had pulled her to a standing position she let go and dropped her glance to the ground. Joseph guessed that he was a good six or seven inches taller than she was. He stared at her bowed head for a moment, watching her try to regain her composure.

"What's your name?" he asked.

She looked up at him, and replied, "Binta, Massa."

"Binta," he repeated. It sounded like one of the African names some of the slaves insisted on using. He looked at the girl's tear-streaked face. Her full lips still quivered slightly but some spirit had returned to the dark brown eyes which she now turned up to him, almost boldly. He frowned slightly. Somehow, she looked familiar. "You work in the great house, don't you?"

"Yes, Massa."

"So what were you doing all the way down here?"

"Mother Dinah sen' me to the stream to get the clothes she leave to dry on the rocks. I was on me way when Massa Johnson grab me arm and drag me into de bushes. I try to fight," her nostrils flared in anger, but then she sighed, "but it was no use. Him too strong an'…him say him would whip me if I fight."

Joseph was silent. He was no fool. He was aware that these things happened on the plantation. Still, he had been shocked to actually witness it. What made it worse, this slave girl looked so young.

"How old are you?" His voice was harsh.

"Massa?" The question seemed to take her by surprise.

"How old are you, Binta?"

"I think…" She hesitated then she said, "Fourteen, Massa."

He bit his lip and frowned. He had actually thought that she was older, maybe fifteen or sixteen. Even through the coarse shift she wore he could see that her body had blossomed. He wondered if Negro girls matured earlier than white ones. He had heard it said that they were a loose lot, unencumbered by thoughts of chastity and morals – there was still too much of Africa in them. There they ran wild and mated whenever and with whomever struck their fancy. Perfect for practice when you want to learn to be a man, some of the boys at school had laughed. They, too, were sons of West Indian planters, and they laughed at his lack of experience in a land of plenty.

He looked sternly at the girl and asked, "Has this happened before?"

"No, Massa. First time."

He stared hard at her and she lowered her eyes. Finally, he spoke. "Get yourself together. We're going back to the house."

Joseph climbed the stairs, bird cage in hand, and headed for the room at the end of the hall. It was Thursday afternoon and Binta would be in the sewing room, as usual. It had been four weeks since the incident with Frederick Johnson. Since then he and Binta had developed a friendship of sorts, much to Joseph's surprise. He had little in common with this slave girl who spoke little but gobbled up anything he chose to share with her. Sometimes he would give her titbits about England and she would sit wide-eyed, seeming almost entranced by his stories. Other times he would leave her to her work while he read or simply lounged in a nearby couch.

When he got to the room he pushed the door open without knocking and went over to sit by the window. He placed the bird cage on the window seat beside him then looked at Binta, who had glanced up from her work when he walked in. She smiled broadly when she saw the two mangoes he rested on the windowsill. She nodded then turned her eyes back to her sewing. He looked at the bowed head in its familiar yellow wrap and smiled.

Joseph put his feet up on the window seat, relaxed, and stared out at the scene below. In the distance the fields of sugar cane were a sea of green under the endless blue of a cloudless sky. Closer to the plantation house Joseph could see black people clothed in dark blue and khaki, slaves bending and chopping at stalks of cane. It was a hot, windless day and he watched as the unforgiving sun baked the already black skin of the men, women and children.

Suddenly, he drew in a sharp breath. One of the labourers had stumbled and fallen. Before the man could rise a white man was on top of him with a whip. He lifted it and brought it down several times and the man on the ground writhed in pain. Another white man rode up on a horse and barked orders. The whipping ended. The slave struggled to his feet, picked up his scythe and bent again to his task. None of the other slaves had stopped for even a moment when the man fell under the foreman's whip. No one acknowledged him when he regained his place among the crew.

Joseph released his breath slowly. He took his feet off the window seat and, turning his back on the scene, rested them on the ground. Binta had rested her sewing in her lap and was looking at him quizzically. He avoided her gaze. He turned to the bird cage, opened it, and gently took the canary on his finger. It immediately flew off, circling the room twice, then perched on top of the armoire.

Both Joseph and Binta looked up at the bird then Joseph said, "He came up to the house, didn't he?"

"Yes, Massa Joe, but him no mess with me."

"You're sure?"

"Yes, Massa, I tell you the truth."

Joseph frowned as he watched Binta's face. The girl averted her eyes and concentrated on the shirt she was mending. He could see that something had made her nervous. "Binta, is there something you are not telling me?"

The girl tightened her lips then spoke, her voice cracking, "Yes, Massa…dere is someting else."

"Yes?" Joseph's voice came out sharper than he had intended. "What is it?"

"I…I…" She shook her head. "Nothing, Massa."

"It can't be 'nothing'. You look afraid. You have to tell me what is bothering you."

"Massa, me want tell you…" Binta's eyes were pleading. "…but me can't. I sorry to trouble you, sah."

"Binta," Joseph's voice became gentle as he tried to reassure her, "tell me what's wrong. I'm sure I can help." When she looked hesitant he continued, "Just trust me."

Her timid eyes suddenly blazed with anger. "I don' trust no white man. You all be like Massa Johnson."

As soon as the words were out Binta clapped a hand over her mouth, eyes wide. "Massa," she whispered, "I sorry, sah. I never mean to say dat." Distress clouded her eyes and a hiccup escaped her lips. "Please don't whip me, Massa. I sorry for what I say." Quick tears filled her eyes.

Shocked by her vehement response Joseph could only stare at the tearful girl. Finally, he said, "Stop crying, Binta. I'm not going to have you whipped. You know that."

She wiped her cheek with the back of her hand and sniffed, but said nothing. Finally, she whispered, "Yes, Massa."

Joseph opened his mouth to say something else but then thought better of it. He turned back to the open window and stared outside, grimfaced. From the corner of his eye he saw the girl bend her head once again to the shirt in her hand. Suddenly she gave a yelp.

"What is it?" Joseph turned quickly at the sound.

"I…I just prick me finger." She flashed her left hand up and down while making a hissing sound through her teeth.

"Let me see." Joseph went over and took her hand. A tiny ball of blood was on her thumb.

"It not too bad now, sah. Is jus' dat de needle did go down deep." She tried to pull her hand away but he held her wrist in a firm grip. She raised nervous eyes to his but he simply wiped the blood away with his thumb.

"It's okay, Binta." He grinned at her. "You'll live."

At that moment the door swung open and Rachel Gordon walked in. "What is going on here?" Her eyes narrowed as she stared at the two. "Joseph, what are you doing in the sewing room? What business do you have with this girl?"

Joseph quickly dropped Binta's hand and stepped back a pace. "Uh, nothing…"

"And you! You've been up here all morning. Get yourself down to the kitchen – now!"

Binta dropped her sewing and as she scurried out of the room Rachel Gordon turned to Joseph. "Don't you know you should not be fraternizing with the slaves?"

"Mother…"

"Your father and I have spoken to you about this before, Joseph. There is a line of separation between us and our slaves. They are not our equals. I don't know why you insist on this foolish behaviour."

"But I wasn't doing anything."

"That is irrelevant. You need to let slaves know their place, and their place is not in the company of their master."

"But I'm not the master," Joseph said weakly.

"One day you will be. Don't ever forget that."

Gathering her skirts around her Rachel turned and swept out of the room. Joseph could still hear her scolding voice as she walked down the hallway. He knew this was not the end of it. She was certain to tell his father and then he would have to endure another lecture at dinnertime.

With a sigh he sat down heavily on the chair that Binta had just vacated. He kicked the shirt which had fallen to the floor, leaned back and groaned. He sat for a while with his eyes closed. Finally, he rose and picked up the bird cage. At his whistle Jack left his perch and flew down into the waiting cage. Joseph slammed the door shut, lifted the cage and walked out the door.

Despite his parents' reprimands Joseph still managed to maintain contact with Binta. He sneaked up to the sewing room every now and then, and once he even convinced her to watch the game with him.

While they sat watching the boys and eating sweet sugar cane she pointed out the hut where she lived with her mother, Mama Pearl. She mentioned, too, that she would be turning fifteen soon – December seventeen, she said.

From the moment Binta told him Joseph thought of surprising her with a gift. He knew immediately what he would give her. Like many of the slaves on the plantation Binta walked barefoot. Shoes were considered a luxury and those who had a pair treasured them. He knew that she would be delighted.

December seventeen finally arrived. He planned to sneak out of the house when the family was asleep and go all the way to the slave village to deliver his gift. He had been there several times over the last few months but never at night. However, it could not be avoided. He had not seen her for the past few weeks and when he enquired about her he was told that she had been sent to the fields. They were busy in the fields and all available hands were needed.

Still, Joseph could not help wondering if his mother had been behind it. Lately, Rachel seemed to be watching him like a hawk and it made him wonder if, somehow, she had found out that he still spent time with the girl. He could not risk her thwarting his plan – not today. He would just have to wait a few more hours until they had all turned in for the night then he would go. He was determined to deliver Binta's gift on her birthday. Feigning a headache, he headed up to his room right after dinner and waited patiently.

By the time the house was finally silent it was almost ten o'clock. He waited another half hour then, gathering up a small canvas bag, slowly opened his bedroom door. The hallway was in darkness. He pulled the door shut behind him, tiptoed down the wide mahogany staircase and headed for the back door. Slowly, very slowly, he pushed the heavy door. Finally, he had it just wide enough to slip through. He gently pulled it shut behind him, ran across the wide verandah then headed for the shelter of the nearby trees. The moon was almost full and Joseph was grateful for the light.

The night air was cool and crickets were chirping in the trees. Tree frogs added their noise to the din for he disturbed their slumber as he ran. Joseph hardly noticed this symphony of the night. His thoughts were on Binta and how she would react when he presented the gift. He knew that she would never believe he had remembered her birthday, and even if he had, he guessed that she would not think that he would have even bothered to get her a gift. A smile crossed his face as he ran. He was looking forward to the surprise.

He crept stealthily past the barracoons and soon came to the rows of huts where he forced himself to take slow, deep breaths. Walking slowly he approached Binta's hut. He was almost at the door when a big, broad woman suddenly stepped out of the shadows. Joseph jumped then calmed down when he heard her voice.

"Massa Joseph. Is dat you?"

"Mama Pearl. Yes, it's me." Joseph took a step closer to the stout woman. "I'm here to see Binta. I know it's late but I need to see her. Is she asleep?"

Mama Pearl's eyes narrowed and she sucked in her breath. "Massa Joseph, it very late."

"I know but I want to talk to her. I won't stay long." Joseph took a step closer but the woman moved to stand in front of the door, arms folded over her bosom. He looked at her, surprised. He knew Mama Pearl was a strong, determined woman but he was the master's son. Why would she try to stop him from entering?

"Massa Joseph, me can't let you go in, sah. Binta not going see you tonight."

Joseph stared at her, confused. The woman stared back at him stubbornly.

"Why don't you want me to see her? It will only be for a minute."

"No, Massa Joseph. No more question, sah. Enough. No more tonight." She shook her heavy head.

Something in the woman's eyes made Joseph uneasy. Her words, somehow, made his heart beat faster. He sensed that something was wrong. "What's going on? Is she ill?"

He tried to force his way past the large woman but she backed up against the door and whispered forcefully, "Massa Joseph, I say no Binta tonight!"

Joseph pretended to turn away but as the woman relaxed her body he swung back and shoved her away. She stumbled and almost fell but he had no time to concern himself with that. He pushed against the flimsy door, calling out as he entered, "Binta! Are you alright?" The shack was in darkness except for a single candle which flickered behind a thin curtain. Joseph headed towards it.

"Binta," he whispered as he tiptoed towards the curtain and gently drew the cloth aside, "it's me."

He got no further. Joseph's eyes opened wide and he gasped as a large man jumped off the sprawled body of the young girl. The white man turned his bearded face to Joseph and they both stared at each other in shock. It was Adam Gordon who looked back at Joseph, his usually ruddy face now chalk-white.

"Joseph! What are you doing here?"

Joseph stared open-mouthed at his father who was now struggling to pull on his breeches. He swung his eyes to look at the dark-skinned girl who lay frozen on the bed. As his eyes raked her face she pulled a thin, rough sheet over her naked body then covered her face with her hands and began to sob.

With a snarl of disgust Joseph threw the canvas bag straight at the weeping girl. He turned and ran from the hut, the picture of his father's half-naked body still imprinted on his mind.

Over an hour passed before Joseph could stomach returning to his room. He sat on the bed, his face in his hands, hurt and disappointment washing over him. After what seemed an eternity he got up and took the cloth off Jack's cage. He smiled wryly at the bird and said softly, "Serves me right, Jack. What else can you expect from those people, anyway?"

Years later Joseph Gordon lay in his four poster canopy bed. The warm night air passed over his naked chest. When his restless body could take it no longer he turned slowly to his wife who lay sleeping deeply. At thirty-two years old he had already been married nine years. His wife had borne him two beautiful daughters but she had become contented with plantation life and was rarely interested in anything sexual. He sighed in frustration.

As the light snores escaped his wife's throat Joseph slowly rolled out of the bed, slipped into his shirt and gathered up his boots. Twenty minutes later he was lying on top of a slim, black body which writhed under his own. The girl strained against him and whispered "No, Massa," but he gripped her shoulders, shoved her back into the pillows and forced her legs apart. The act was over quickly.

As he lay spent, the faint memory of the dark brown eyes of a long-departed slave girl pierced his heart – a girl who had once been his friend. A bitter taste filled his mouth. He had become his father. With a groan, almost of pain, he pushed himself out of the bed, dressed quickly and walked out into the tropical night.

Chapter 2

1839

Creamy sat under the mango tree, scrubbing the heavy iron pot. The red sun was still low in the sky and he shivered in the cold, clean air. He had burnt the cornmeal porridge. Again. After scrubbing a moment longer he hissed through his teeth and threw it down in the grass, frustrated. No amount of scrubbing was going to make it look any better. He marvelled at the way his mother had been able to keep the cooking vessels and utensils sparkling. He was a strong, twenty-five year old man and he could not do it. How did she, small as she was?

Creamy stood slowly, his knees creaking, then put his hands to his spine and leaned back in a long stretch. He yawned long and wide. He had been up most of the night tending to his mother and could do with some sleep. Although he was tired he had risen very early to make sure that she had some food in her stomach. He wanted her to have a good day. He rubbed his eyes, sniffed the crisp morning air then shuffled back into the shack.

As soon as he entered he heard the laboured breathing of his mother who lay on the narrow bed in the corner. She stirred then spoke weakly. "Zeke? You finish already?"

"Yeah, Ma. Me wasn't doing too good on that pot so me just give up."

He went over to her but she had closed her eyes again. He stood there for a long while staring at the shrunken mummy that had once been his mother. For the past two years he had watched her slowly declining, changing from the vibrant and cheerful woman he had known to this sick, shrunken creature.

He remembered the days not so long ago when he and his mother used to play like children in the yard. Once, she even beat him to the top of a tree to pick a ripe mango. One would never believe that at the time she was thirty-eight years old. She was a grown woman with an adult son but she was young at heart and childlike in many ways.

Now she lay in her corner, a mere shell of the woman she used to be. Apart from her distended belly her emaciated body was like a skeleton. Because of her illness she could only keep down soft foods. Meals of rice and peas and meat were substituted with soup or porridge. Maybe it was a good thing that was all she could stomach anyway, Creamy thought, because lately there had been no money for anything else. Right now they were just barely surviving.

The house was a mess. He had not been paying attention to it these past few days. He had been so preoccupied with trying to make life bearable for her that he had not even noticed that things were piling up. Clothes were strewn all over the dirt floor and plates and cups were piled high in a tin bucket. Suddenly he felt that he had to get things in order or he would go mad.

He grabbed the bucket and made for the door. There was a loud crash. Plastic cups and tin plates scattered everywhere. The woman in the bed jerked upright and opened startled, sunken eyes.

"Sorry, Ma," Creamy said quickly, "the handle give way."

"Why you so clumsy, bwoy?" Her voice was a hoarse, breathless growl. "You can't give me a chance to rest?"

Creamy bit his lip and gathered up the plates and cups from the ground. He knew that his mother was simply venting her pain and frustration on him. After two years he was almost used to it. He went out and deposited the bucket beside the pot he had thrown down by the mango tree.

Creamy let out a sigh then walked slowly to the back of the shack. He had saved a couple of pieces of corn pone for the dog. As he threw the scraps of food at the scrawny animal he spoke apologetically.

"Hey, boy. Me know you hungry but this all me have."

The dog gobbled up the food in one bite and wagged his tail wildly, eagerly awaiting more. He strained at the rope around his neck and yelped at his master.

"Calm down, boy." Creamy stooped down and rubbed the dog's head. "I goin' get you more later, Pitchy-Patchy. Jus' drink some water for now." He pushed the enamel pan under the dog's nose and watched him lap thirstily.

Creamy smiled as he remembered how the dog had ended up with that name. When he was just a pup Pitchy-Patchy knocked over a pail of white lime which was being used to whitewash the roots of coconut trees to ward off insects. White lime flew everywhere and when the dog ran off he was splattered in white. For days he ran around with white patches on his black body. Even when the white was all gone the name remained.

Creamy's face sobered as he remembered how he, too, had been saddled with a nickname because he was different. He had been only six years old when the other slave boys started calling him "Creamy". His olive skin and wavy black hair made it obvious that his father was not of the Negro race. "Your coffee have in too much cream," they would laugh and Creamy would go off by himself to cry. He would ask his mother who his father was but he never got an answer. All she ever said was that they had each other and that was all that mattered.

As Creamy got older he learned to ignore the taunts of the other slave boys and he even made friends with a few of them. Still, they never let him forget that he was different. Over the years he learned to deal with his loneliness by relying on his mother for the friendship he craved. When he became a teenager his relationship with his mother grew even stronger because then he could really speak to her about his thoughts, his feelings, his problems. At that time he felt that he could survive without the rest of them. But when he got older and physical urges became a part of his life he realized that he could not survive alone. His relationship with his mother was not enough. He'd had a few encounters with women while he lived on the slave plantation but none since he left the estate over a year ago.

Although the slaves were emancipated in 1834 he still had to serve four years of apprenticeship to the Williams family. When full abolition came in 1838 he found himself a free man at the age of twenty-four. He remembered his elation at finally being free. The whole country was in an uproar. Young black men and women were eager to start their lives in freedom. There were celebrations all over the island.

But now, looking back, he wondered if this freedom was real. It was physical freedom, yes, but he felt as if he were still under the control of the plantation owners. Being a free man without education, without skills other than chopping sugar cane, was almost worse than being a slave. At least while he was a slave he had a roof over his head and regular meals. Now it was a struggle to find the next meal and, with his mother sick, the situation was even worse. She needed medication - lots of it - and he had no money. He hated to see her suffer day after day. They could no longer depend on the kindness of neighbours to keep them going. He had to do something…fast.

Next morning Creamy stood shivering in the chill air. It was still not yet five o'clock but already several men had gathered at the gate of Innswood Estate. Unemployment was a crisis on the island and, like Creamy, there were thousands of ex-slaves looking for work. The situation was desperate for many of them because they had no option outside of working in the fields. Many of the planters had gone back to England once slavery was abolished. Because of that the few plantations that were hiring workers were bombarded. Creamy knew that the chances that he would be hired were slim but he had to try. His mother was back at home waiting for him and she needed food and medicine. He would do anything in his power for her.

The foreman did not come to the gate until seven that morning and by that time Creamy had been standing for over two hours. The morning had warmed up considerably and he was feeling much more comfortable.

He always loved the sun, not only for its warmth and because it darkened his skin, but because it seemed to keep him in a positive mood. Even in his darkest moments the brightness of a sunny day always seemed to make him see the brighter side of any situation.

By this time over sixty or seventy men were standing at the gate, all waiting hopefully for a job. Some of them stared questioningly at him while others glared openly but he tried not to pay attention to them. He knew what he was there for. Still, it was difficult to ignore them.

One of them said, in a very audible voice, "What de hell him doing here? Him no should be on de other side o' de fence?"

There was some grumbling among some of the men but Creamy tried to deafen his ears to it. He knew they resented his light skin and his presence at the gate. He was competition because he could possibly take one of the few places available for work. He knew that they thought he had more privileges than they did, but this was not the case. The fact was, regardless of his lighter skin, with no education he had no advantage over the black men who stood beside him. He was just as much a slave to his situation as they were. Creamy closed his ears to the jeers, hardened his heart to the pain, and stood silent.

As the gate opened they made a move to rush forward but the foreman held up his hand, rifle above his head, and shouted, "Hold on! Only need fifteen today." A universal groan went up as the men realized how slim their chances were.

"Stand back. All of you!"

As they backed up the foreman stepped forward, glaring at the men in front of him. He pointed a grimy finger at the largest of the group.

"You. Go stand over there."

As he pointed to the spot the black man moved forward, a smirk on his face. The foreman continued the process of selection until all fifteen stood before him. Disappointment was heavy in his heart as Creamy turned with the rest of the rejected men and slowly walked away.

Back in his village that evening Creamy sat on a boulder on the bank of the White River and stared into the muddy green water. He needed to gather his thoughts.

He had just had a long conversation with his mother and they had made some serious decisions. She desperately needed help and he was her only source of support. Although she wanted him near and he would have preferred to be by her side they knew that a parting would be inevitable. This was the only way he could help her. He had tried his best to find employment right there in the community but nothing had worked so far. The competition was too tight.

He and his mother spoke about that plantation on which she had grown up so many years ago, the one all the way on the western side of the island. Life there had not been bad, she said, and even when slaves had starved on other plantations during the bad times when foreign trade was affected by the American War she had always had food to eat.

Now he was considering leaving her, travelling almost a hundred miles to get back to this plantation, to find a way to survive. The plan was for him to try to secure a job there, stay for the entire cane cutting season, if possible, and negotiate for some time in-between to come and visit her. He was not totally comfortable leaving his mother in the care of neighbours but it was the best he could do.

He got up from the boulder and walked slowly back to the shack. The skinny dog tied to the post yelped in eager anticipation but Creamy's face remained serious this time. He bent and loosened the knot in the rope and gave the dog a quick pat on the head. He had never been able to feed the animal properly and he knew that there were other people in the community who would throw scraps to him. He would survive. He slapped the dog hard on the rump and watched him run away.

On Monday morning Creamy was up before there was any hint of sunlight. He hurriedly packed a canvas sack with pieces of bread, 'turn cornmeal' and a bottle of water. He had a long journey ahead of him and no money to buy food so he had to be prepared. He did not know what today would bring but he was counting on luck smiling down on him. He was taking the last few coins that were in the house to pay for his passage to Negril and although he knew there was no certainty that he would find work, somehow he felt positive.

"Mama, I going now." He spoke softly in the stillness of the early morning.

"Zeke, come here, boy."

"Yes, Ma?"

"Zeke…I got something to tell you. 'Bout dat plantation."

Creamy winced as his mother groaned in pain. Her voice was almost a whisper.

"Don't talk now, Ma," he begged. "Just rest."

"Ezekiel, maybe me no see you again…" The speech was cut short by a violent fit of coughing.

"Mama, don't talk, please. I know. You tell me already to be careful of people, that them not always what them appear to be. Me remember everything you tell me, Mama." The woman in the bed could only continue to cough. Finally, she stared up at her son with watery eyes and nodded. Talking was now out of the question. Once she had her coughing fit she was too weak to even whisper.

Creamy gathered her in his arms, hugged her gently then laid her back in the bed. A tear rolled down one cheek as he stared at his once beautiful mother then he leaned forward and whispered, "I going now, Mama. I going to get Jean to come stay with you right now." Then he turned and, without looking back, picked up his canvas sack, went through the door and pulled it shut behind him.

There were four of them on the cart headed for the west - Creamy, an old woman and her grandson, and a girl who may have been in her late teens. The old woman and the boy dozed quietly. The driver was silent as he flicked his whip from time to time at the rump of the mule. Creamy and the young woman sat at the very back of the cart, dozing.

They were almost an hour into their journey before the morning started to warm up. Creamy opened his eyes, rubbed away the last vestiges of sleep and breathed in the crisp morning air. He looked at the sun just beginning to rise over the hills. It was a beautiful morning. The sky had no blue in it, only red, orange and yellow hues that made it look like a painter's canvas.

As the cart trundled along the dirt road the dew on the bushes and trees made the green leaves glisten and the warmth of the early morning sun gently baked Creamy's skin and lifted his spirits. With a slight smile he turned to look at the girl who sat beside him, her head resting against a sack full of cabbages. Her eyes were still closed but Creamy felt the urge to talk and he wondered if he should wake her. This was totally uncharacteristic of him but today was different from any other day. It almost felt like the day he was freed from slavery. On an impulse, he touched the girl's arm and said, "Hey."

With a groan and a slight stretch the girl slowly straightened her body and opened her eyes. She turned her face towards Creamy and then a questioning look entered her eyes.

"Is you wake me up?"

"Yeah. Sorry, but me think you would get crick in your neck. You never look too comfortable."

The girl rubbed the back of her neck and stifled a yawn.

"You right," she groaned. "Me neck feel stiff." Then, looking around her, she asked, "Where we are?"

"We jus' pass Discovery Bay."

"After all this time, das all?"

"Yeah," Creamy smiled. "This not exactly the queen's carriage. One lickle mule can't go so fast."

The girl smiled back, her tiny white teeth glistening behind full lips. Creamy stared at her and, before he could stop himself, he asked, "What you name?"

"Elizabeth," she replied.

"Elizabeth? You have fancy name."

The girl ducked her head shyly then looked up at him and said, "My mother say she name me after a white girl because I jus' as good as them." She lifted dark eyes, almost defiantly, and stared straight at Creamy. He looked back at her admiringly. This petite ebony-skinned girl was probably as poor as he was but seemed so proud.

"You make a fine Elizabeth," he grinned.

"And what you name?"

"Crea… Aah, Ezekiel."

"Crezekiel? What kinda name is that?"

He laughed out loud then looked back down at her, still chuckling with amusement.

"No, me name Ezekiel, after the man in the Bible. But from I was a pickney them call me Creamy."

"Why? You drink a lot of cream?"

Creamy shook his head. "No, them call me so because of my skin."

"Oh," said the girl, looking him up and down, seeming to notice his paleness for the first time. "And you don't mind that name?"

Creamy was taken aback by her question and quickly answered, "Yes, but…that is what they call me."

"Well, if I don't want people to call me by a name they can't because I would never answer them." The girl looked at him, a hint of stubbornness on her face. "You say you Mama name you Ezekiel after a man in the Bible. Don't you think that was for a reason?"

"It don't matter…"

The girl cut him off, "Yes, it do matter! If my Mama did name me Ezekiel after somebody in the Bible then I would think that is a special name. And nobody could call me no nickname either."

Creamy felt his face get hot and he looked down at the rough road. Somehow, he felt ashamed. This skinny young girl was more of a man than he was. She was proud of her name and felt he should be proud of his, too. Their mothers had given them special names and yet all he was to the people in his community was Creamy - not black, not white, but a blend of the two that only brought him rejection from both sides.

He shook his head then turned to look into the girl's defiant eyes. He said nothing. Instead, he nodded his head slowly then turned his gaze back to the dirt road as it disappeared slowly while they trundled along. He knew what he should do. He was not going to try to be on either one side or the other. He would be true only to himself. From here on, he resolved, he would be none other than Ezekiel.

For the next six hours Elizabeth and Ezekiel enjoyed each other's company and conversation. The old woman and the young boy had, by this time, woken up. As the eleven o'clock sun hit their bare heads the woman pulled out a basket full of mangoes and oranges. She even had a whole roasted breadfruit and pieces of red herring in her basket. To the surprise of the two young people she placed the basket in the middle of the wagon and invited them to partake. Elizabeth's delight was obvious as she grabbed a Julie Mango from the top of the pile. She bit into it and juice spurted out, some of it hitting Creamy on the forehead. He laughed, wiped it away, then reached into the basket and took an orange for himself.

It was almost five o'clock in the evening when the cart finally arrived in Negril. The old woman and the boy had already gotten off in Montego Bay but Ezekiel and Elizabeth had remained on the cart. He learned, with some surprise and much pleasure, that they were both on the way to the same plantation. A friend had recommended her for a job as a nursemaid for twin babies who had recently been born. They got off the cart and walked to the gate together.

It was September and five weeks had passed since Ezekiel had been hired on the plantation. The work was hard. He was up before dawn every day and chopped cane until the set of sun. Sometimes he was assigned to night duty at the boiling house where the stalks of cane were put through the huge sugar mill so that the sweet juice could be extracted and collected in huge kettles and boiled. The steam from the mill, the heat of the furnace and the overly sweet odour of boiling cane juice always made Ezekiel slightly nauseous. He was relieved when he was sent back to the field.

So far he had been able to send money home twice and he got word that, with the medicine, his mother was showing signs of improvement. He had not been able to return for a visit but he planned to talk to the foreman to see if he could get three days off in the coming week. He would have to negotiate this one. He had gotten into a fight the week before and the foreman had come down hard on him even though he had sworn it was not his fault. He seemed to have made enemies of two men who constantly taunted him, and the one time he dared throw angry words back at them they had attacked him. After that he stayed out of their way and kept his mouth shut.

As Ezekiel lay on the bed his thoughts ran back to his village. He recalled the days right after emancipation when everyone had had so much hope for the future. Freedom was sweet on the tongue in those days when they still had thoughts of prosperity and happiness. But those dreams had soon been tempered with reality. Over a year later he had not accomplished much. But this job was the light at the end of the tunnel. It was back-breaking work but he was good at it and the wages were reasonable. He finally felt that he would make it.

Then his world turned upside down.

One night, soon after completing his sixth week, Creamy left the other men at the canteen and dragged himself back to the sleeping quarters, exhausted. It had been a long day and he was too tired to eat. He was just drifting into sleep when a shout outside jerked him wide awake. The door to the sleeping quarters flew open and the foreman walked in.

"You, boy, get up right now!"

Ezekiel rose from the bed slowly, blinking. He was groggy and confused.

"Yes, Mr. Robinson?" His voice was scratchy with sleep. "What's the problem, sah?"

"You know what the problem is. Come with me."

Ezekiel frowned but without another word he put on his boots, grabbed his khaki work shirt and followed the foreman out into the chilly night. His heart pounded but he tried to keep calm. He wanted to ask the foreman if this had something to do with his mother but he was too afraid to utter a word. He did not want to hear the worst. They arrived at the estate office and Peter Robinson pulled the door open and stepped inside. Ezekiel was right behind him.

As soon as the foreman went over to the desk two black men stepped out of the shadows. Ezekiel stopped short and stared at them. This could not be news about his mother. He recognized these men and they knew nothing about her. They were the same ones with whom he had fought. He was filled with a sense of foreboding because he knew that nothing good was going to come out of this meeting.

The foreman stood behind his desk and looked at him. "Hubert and Casey, here, say they know who stole the money that disappeared from my office."

Ezekiel drew in a shaky breath but said nothing.

"It was you."

"Mr. Robinson, why you say this?" Ezekiel's voice sounded shrill even to his own ears. "I don't know nothing 'bout no money."

"Really, now? Casey, let's hear it."

The shorter of the two men took a step forward and, without looking at Ezekiel, said to the foreman, "Yes, boss, is like we tell you. We see him sneaking out that same night."

"You see me?" Ezekiel's voice trembled. "What a lying…"

"There were two witnesses." The foreman glared at Ezekiel with a look of disgust. "Don't even try to deny it."

"Yes, boss. We see him, yes. Him did have a black bag in him hand."

Ezekiel took a step back and shook his head in shock.

"Where do you think you're going?" The foreman stepped forward and the two men followed.

"I…I jus' don't believe dis."

Ezekiel's heart raced as the horror of the situation filled his mind. He could be locked up for a long time for a crime he did not commit, and only on the testimony of two men who hated him.

He spoke with urgency. "Boss, please. Is all a lie. These men hate me. Them hate me ever since I come to this plantation. Don't believe them, boss. Give me a chance!"

"A chance to do what? Bring the money back?"

"No, boss! I don't know nothing 'bout no money. Give me a chance to prove that me innocent."

"You think I am an idiot, boy?" The foreman's voice

was a growl. He looked at Ezekiel's accusers and shouted, "Hold him, boys! Don't let him run off."

Before Ezekiel could move the men were on top of him, wrestling him to the ground.

As he fell under their weight his head bumped on the floor - hard.

Ezekiel woke up in a dank, dark cell that he knew had held wayward slaves in the past. The shackles and chains were still embedded in the walls but he lay on the ground, unfettered. That was small consolation to him because if he did not find a way to prove his innocence he could end up in prison for years, denying his mother her last chance at life.

The next time he woke it was to the sound of someone calling his name. With a jerk he opened his eyes and sat up. His body was cramped from sleeping on the cold, hard ground and his stomach growled from lack of food. Although he could see the sunlight through the narrow slits at the top of the wall it was dark inside the cell and, as his eyes focused, he just barely made out the form of a woman standing over him.

"Ezekiel," she said softly.

He knew that voice. It was Elizabeth.

"What you doing here?"

"The whole plantation hear about what happen last night. I bring you some food."

"They let you in here?"

"They know you can't escape. Men outside the door, anyway."

Ezekiel gratefully took the tray from Elizabeth's hands and surveyed the fare. Boiled green bananas, callaloo and fried plantains were on the plate. His stomach growled in anticipation. He picked up the fork, cut into one of the bananas, and gobbled it down greedily.

"You bring any coffee?"

"Boy, not even a thanks for the food and you demanding coffee."

There was a smile in Elizabeth's voice as she knelt down on the floor beside Ezekiel and handed him a mug. The strong scent of coffee hit his nose, perking him up instantly.

"I make it black. That's how you like it?"

"That's exactly how I like it," he said as he looked her up and down with a crooked grin. He cleaned his plate quickly then handed the tray back to Elizabeth who sat on the floor beside him, her arms around her knees, watching.

"What you goin' do?"

"Bwoy, I don't know. This is a hell of a thing to get out of."

"Just tell them the truth."

"You don't think I been doing that all this time? When you have people who hate you just because of your skin colour is a hell of a thing."

"I know the man them that accuse you. But you know what? I believe the foreman have something against you, too."

"Why you say dat?"

"You don't think that him believe them a little bit too easy? I believe seh because him have a touch of black in him, him have a chip on him shoulder. You don't think so?"

"How you know him have black in him? An' furthermore, what dat have to do with me?"

"Bwoy, you doan know how this worl' run? I feel that the man look on you and almost see himself because jus' one touch more o' black blood and him would be in the fields cutting cane like youself. Next time you see him look on him nose good." She grinned. "You ever see a backra with a nose broad like that?"

"You thinking deep, girl." Ezekiel grinned back. "Maybe too deep."

"Well, you might think so, but I know what I am saying. But back to your problem. What you goin' do?"

"I was going to appeal to the foreman again. But since you think him might not like me that plan don't seem to make much sense anymore. Now I don't know what to do."

Elizabeth rubbed her eyes then spoke slowly. "I think your best chance is to appeal to the Busha. Go past this foreman and appeal to the real boss. I hear him can be a fair man."

"An' how the hell you expect me to get to the plantation owner? See me here, lock in the cell. You goin' free me to go see him?"

"Well, I can't free you but I can get a message to him."

"How?"

"Remember, I work in the big house and I see the family everyday. You forget is I look after the children? I can put a case to him wife and ask her to present it to him. She a nice lady. She will listen."

"I will take anything you can do to help me, girl. But I still don't know how I would prove that is not me take the thing."

"Well, I was thinking…I will tell them that you was with me that night. We can tell them that we friendly from long time. Remember, them see we come here together."

"But that not true. What if you get in trouble?"

"An' de man them what frame you, them not telling truth neither. So why you care 'bout that? Anyway, you have any better idea?"

Ezekiel was silent then he said, "No. I can't think of a thing."

"Well, then…" Elizabeth rose, tray in hand, "…we have a plan."

She smiled at him then slipped back through the door, pulling it shut behind her.

Later that day as Ezekiel sat in the dark in nervous anticipation he heard the door to the cell open. A burly black man entered the room. It was the foreman's assistant.

"Come with me," was all he said then he turned and strode out of the room. Ezekiel had to rise quickly and hurry after him.

When they got to the great house he was taken through a side door into a room that looked like a library. Books lined several shelves. At the back of the room there was a huge desk strewn with papers. There was no one in the room.

The man shoved him inside then slammed the door shut leaving Ezekiel to stand alone, confused. Within moments the door opened again and this time a tall, lanky white man wearing a broad straw hat entered, Elizabeth trailing behind him.

"So…what is this I hear about money missing from my foreman's office?"

As he spoke the man removed his hat and turned to face Ezekiel. His thin face was tanned and his brown hair was greying at the temples. He pushed his spectacles higher up his nose and rested calm, brown eyes on Ezekiel. The man looked him over, a slightly questioning look in his eyes. "Liz, here, has been trying to give me some other story about the incident. Now you tell me what happened."

Ezekiel's heart pounded in his chest. He knew this was his last chance. He looked at Elizabeth who stared calmly back at him and was comforted by her strength. Taking a deep breath, he began to speak. He explained how he had been picked on by the two men who accused him, then went on to describe a night spent in the arms of Elizabeth. He spoke with confidence and as he continued he began to relax in the owner's presence.

The man listened without interrupting and Ezekiel felt that he might have finally found a sympathetic ear. At one point he became a little uncomfortable when Elizabeth kept staring at him then at the white man, but he kept on talking.

"Missah Gordon, I would never steal from you, sah. This work is what is keeping me mother alive. She in a bad way, sah. This the only way I can get her medicine."

"I'm sorry to hear that." The man's voice was quiet but his look was kind.

"I been trying for months now to get work so I could help her and this is the first place that offer me a job. I know this place was right for me, sah, because is me mother tell me about it. She say that things would be better if me come to this same plantation where she born."

"Your mother was born here?"

"Yes, Massa Gordon, sah. She come from right here, but she say when she was a young girl here a white man make her lay down with him. An' then them sell her to another plantation when them find out that she pregnant. Then she have me."

The white man seemed taken aback by his bluntness but, seeing that he had caught the man's interest, Ezekiel pressed on.

"So you see, Massa Gordon, this is like me coming back to me roots. Is here me mother come from and that's why she give me the name Ezekiel Gordon, after this plantation. Me would never rob from the place where me mother born, and me would never rob the place that allow me to get money for her medicine. Me is not a thief, sah."

"You know," the tall white man looked Ezekiel straight in the eyes, "when I first saw you I felt I recognized you from somewhere. You say your mother was from here? What is her name?"

"She name Binta, sah," Ezekiel answered, then frowned at the tears that suddenly appeared in the Busha's eyes.

Chapter 3

1934

Beth looked up at the light-skinned woman who stared coldly at her as she lay down the rules of the house. She was tired. She had awoken at sunrise to catch the country bus to Kingston. She had only had a chance to drink a cup of chocolate tea and grab a piece of bread before she'd had to run down the hill to the dirt road on which the bus passed.

At that hour of the morning the narrow road was almost hidden in thick fog but the driver seemed unperturbed as he revved the engines and drove the rickety bus as fast as it would go. It was Thursday and the vehicle was packed with country people heading for the Coronation Market, their loads of produce piled high on top of the bus. Market women were engaged in animated conversation and, depressed though Beth was, she could not help being entertained by their stories and jokes. For the while their lively chatter took her mind off her own situation but, more importantly, it distracted her enough so that she forgot to stare fearfully out of the window at the steep precipice along which the road ran.

It took three hours around the winding Junction Road to Kingston. When she arrived at Half Way Tree Square she had to walk for twenty minutes before she got to the house. She was hot and thirsty.

As she stood before the lady of the house she wondered if the woman would think her forward if she asked for a drink of water. She peered up at the rigid face and decided against it.

"You are to listen to the cook and make sure you do everything she says." The woman spoke sharply. "You are responsible for the children's clothes and you must get them ready for school every morning."

She pointed to a corner of the living room. "Put your bag down over there and follow me." Without looking back she walked into the kitchen and called, "Mildred!"

Beth dropped her bag in the corner and followed the woman in a daze. She had not yet fully recovered from the shock. It had been three weeks since her mother had called her into the bedroom, sat her down, and told her that she would have to leave. She was third in a family of five children and, at fourteen years old, was already a responsible member of the family. She had been taking care of younger siblings since she was nine. Their father struggled to eke out a living for them from the little field which he cultivated, but it was hard. It was depression time and families all over Jamaica were having a rough time.

A hundred years had passed since the emancipation of Jamaica's slaves and although the current generation knew nothing of slavery, they were all too familiar with the hardships of survival as small farmers in a country faced with economic depression, conflicts over land, and a huge working class struggling for political recognition. Beth had heard her parents talking about Jamaica's problems. Once, when she had been in the field helping them gather the corn, she had heard her father talking about leaving home to join the dock workers. At least there, he had said, with Manley and Bustamante working to form labour unions, things would be better. But although he spoke about it often he never left home, and Beth was glad.

Just before Christmas her mother began hinting that there would have to be some changes around the house if they were to survive. She had mentioned sending one of them to live with distant relatives, but even though Beth had heard her talking about it she had never believed that it would really happen. And to be sent to a total stranger! She was being given away. She could never understand that and she would never forgive her mother. She knew this was not her father's doing. He loved her too much. He said she was his princess. But no matter how hard she cried, when the day came Beth was put on the bus to Kingston. Her mother had cried, too. She had pleaded with Beth to understand and had told her that she was doing what she thought was best for her but all Beth could feel was anger and hurt.

In the kitchen a stout black woman was standing with her back to the door, stirring a heavy cast iron pot on the stove.

"Mildred, did you hear me?" The woman's sharp voice made the stout woman turn quickly.

"Yes Mam?"

"Mildred, this is Beth. She is here from the country. Remember I told you about her?"

"Yes, Mam. The young lady who goin' help me in the kitchen and with the children."

"Same one. Now she's all yours. Make sure she doesn't get into any trouble." With that the woman turned and headed back to the living room.

Wiping her hands in her apron, Mildred said, "Come, child, let me show you where you goin' to sleep."

This was the extent of Beth's welcome to her new home. She ran back to the living room and grabbed her bag. As she trudged behind Mildred towards the helpers' quarters, tears filled her eyes. On hearing her sniff Mildred stopped and, with a look of pity, said to her, "You alright, child?"

Fighting hard to hold back the tears, Beth answered stonily, "Yes, Mam. I am jus' fine."

Although it was just after seven o'clock in the morning Coronation Market was bustling with people. Beth loved to listen to the shouts and laughter of the market people as they tried to sell their foodstuff. They were quick to make conversation with her and their laughter was free and easy. The country-folk had none of the formality and coolness which Beth found in the people of Kingston. On the contrary, with her newly acquired sense of propriety she realized that their openly interested stares and quickness to ask personal questions bordered on rudeness. She loved it. These were her people.

This morning Beth lingered by the pineapple stall, enjoying the fruity fragrance that filled the air and watching the merchant whittling away at a small piece of wood. When he was done he gave her a toothless grin and handed her a tiny wooden bird on a stick. She grinned back at the old man and stuck the bird into a thick plait of her hair. She waved goodbye to the deaf mute then wandered on through the crowd of shoppers. She stepped gingerly around piles of potatoes and oranges as she went on her search for a pumpkin for the Saturday soup. This was one of her few pleasures since she had moved to Kingston - her weekly sojourns to the market.

"Hi, young lady! Come try these nice juicy mangoes, nuh?" A tall, lanky black woman stopped in front of her with a pan piled high with mangoes.

"No, thanks. I have special things I come for today."

Before she had even finished the sentence the woman had already turned away to solicit purchase from another potential customer. "Hi, lady…"

Beth took no offence but turned and pushed though the crowd until she reached the place where Mama Jean sat. The petite old woman was from her very own district of Bonny Gate. It was Mama Jean who had recognized her on her first visit to the market and had called out, "Wait! Is little Beth Gordon, this?"

Beth had smiled broadly in recognition and had reached over to grab the old woman's hands. "Yes, Mama Jean! I livin' in Kingston now!"

"What you saying, girl! You run 'way from country and moving up in life now."

"Well…I not really moving up but I trying to help myself."

"I know how it is, me child. You have to try, you know."

"So how Marse George doing?"

"Him not too bad but him still have the pain a back. Is so it go when you moving up in age."

"Tell him I say I hope him feel better soon. Mama Jean, can I get three pounds of the pumpkin today?"

"Anything for you, me baby."

As Mama Jean cut the pumpkin Beth shifted the heavy bag on her shoulder. Just talking to the old woman took her back to the country, to the smell of the freshly cut grass she would feed the cows, the sound of the birds in the early morning, the taste of ripe June plums that were so sour they made her suck her cheeks in. She missed her older sister's nagging, her older brother's jokes and the little ones who were such a handful.

Beth blinked and stared at the piece of pumpkin in Mama Jean's outstretched hand. She took the food with a quick smile of thanks, handed the money to the woman and hurried on her way.

When Beth turned into the walkway leading up to the house Mrs. Henley was waiting at the front door.

"What do you mean by strolling in here so late?"

The woman's voice was even colder than usual. Her dark eyes flashed and Beth felt a chill run through her body. She knew that the woman had no love for her but she could not understand why she sometimes seemed to hate her. She had taken her into her home, hadn't she? Beth had not asked to come here.

"It's almost ten o'clock. You could not have been at the market all this time. Make sure I don't hear about you hanging around with any boys. Do you think I don't know you young girls these days? As soon as I turn my back you take up with some man." She put her hands on her hips. "Next thing I know, you will be coming in here with a big belly. Don't even think about it! It won't do in this house. Understand?

"Cynthia, why don't you leave the girl alone?"

Mr. Henley sauntered into the kitchen, his paunch preceding him. He was a short, plump white man with a balding head. He was always smiling. He was fat and round and reminded Beth of a rooster, with his big upper body and tiny legs. Although his wife was light-skinned her hair was black and curly, and it could be seen from her skin tone that she was of mixed blood. He, on the other hand, was milk-white with light brown hair. Both of them were born Jamaicans, and it was obvious that they had benefited from the legacy of some old money.

"The girl probably just stopped to greet her friends or something," the man continued. "Isn't that right, aah, what's your name again, honey? Beth?"

She nodded nervously, and he smiled at her.

"Nice name."

"Phillip," Mrs. Henley frowned as she turned to her husband, "you know I don't like it when you interfere with my supervision of the workers."

"Alright, sweetie. You know you're the boss."

With a smile he slid his arm around her waist and gave her a loud kiss on the cheek. Cynthia Henley struggled weakly to get free but a slight smile had already begun to soften her cold lips and it was obvious that her husband had a strong effect on her. He nuzzled her neck with his lips and her body relaxed against him. She gave a soft sigh.

Suddenly, her body went taut again, and she whipped her head around to glare at Beth. "Well, don't just stand there. Go find Mildred and help her with dinner."

Beth needed no further instruction. Without a word she grabbed the bags full of produce and hurried past them. She found Mildred in the backyard sitting on a stool, humming while she vigorously scrubbed the parrot fish to get the scales off.

They exchanged greetings then Beth took some of the food from the bag, washed them then sat on a log beside the cook. She began to peel the green bananas and yams for the evening meal. They worked in silence for a while then Beth dropped her knife into the big pan at her feet and looked at the cook.

"Miss Mildred?"

"Yes, child?"

"You wanted to be a cook all your life?"

Mildred frowned slightly as she looked at Beth. "What you talking 'bout, child?"

"When you was my age, you wanted to be a cook?"

Dropping her own knife into the pan of water and fish Mildred rested her elbows on her knees and said, "Well…by the time I was your age I already know that I couldn't be what I wanted to be."

"What was that?"

Mildred laughed. "I did want to be a secretary."

"A secretary?"

"Yes. I always see them nice looking ladies in them pretty suit and I think secretary job must be a great job. You get to buy a lot of clothes."

"Then why you never become a secretary then?"

"Heh, that is the question. When I get older I get to understand that is only the high-color people alone can be secretary. Look how me black. Them wouldn't want me in them big fancy office."

"And then you decide to be a cook?"

"No, me have other fancy dream to be a nurse or even a singer. I love singing, you know."

Smiling, Beth said, "I know, Miss Mildred. You have a pretty, pretty voice. Is you bring off the choir."

"Thanks, me child."

"But you still don't tell me why you become a cook."

"Is not by choice, me dear, but by the will of God. We was having it rough so me mother get me a position with a white lady in Port Antonio. She was the mayor wife and I was with her eighteen years until she pass away. But before she die she tell her daughter-in-law about me and so that is how I end up at this house. Is about thirteen years I am here now."

"Wow. That is a long time with the mistress."

Both of them burst out laughing. When the laughter died down Beth looked at Mildred and said, "You know what I want to be? A teacher."

"A teacher? That would be a nice job for you. You are a bright girl."

"From I was eight years old I knew I wanted to be a teacher."

"That's nice, child. So you did get plenty schooling when you was in the country?"

"My mother used to pull me from school sometimes to help her in the field but I still study my book. An' Miss Finley, my teacher, used to still send the homework for me to do, even when I didn't make it to class. She nice, you see. Is she why I want to be a teacher."

"Teacher Beth…it sound good," Mildred said proudly.

Beth took up the knife and started to peel bananas again. She did so with such vigour that Mildred said, "Wait! Is fight you fighting the banana them?"

Without looking up at her Beth said, "Miss Mildred, from I come here over a month now Miss Henley don't send me to no school, so how me going to become a teacher?"

"You know, is true. The time fly so fast since you come I didn't even realize that is so long."

"What I goin' to do?" Beth looked at Mildred, distressed.

"Well, the only thing I see you can do is to have a serious talk with Miss Cynthia. You are a hard-working little girl and I don't see why she wouldn't allow you a little time every day to go do your lessons."

"You really think I can talk to her?"

"I know Miss Cynthia is a tough lady but one thing she love is people with ambition. Just make up your mind and talk to her. Nothing try, nothing done, right?"

"Alright, Miss Mildred. I goin' do that."

Feeling more cheerful, Beth continued at her task. She stopped when Mildred spoke again.

"Beth, you know you almost look like Miss Cynthia?"

"Me, Miss Mildred? You don't see that Miss Cynthia look like a white lady?"

"Yes, but she not white, although she really high-color for true. But your skin not dark either, and you have pretty hair. You have Indian in your family?"

"I don't know, but my grandpa was part white. Him grandmother was a black slave woman but him grandfather was a white man."

Mildred looked thoughtful. "Hmm…no, that deh white blood would haffi real strong fi travel so far. You definitely have Indian in you family." Then she said, with interest, "Tell me some more 'bout dis fancy white man in you family."

"Grampy tell me that him grandfather was a big man who did own some plantation or something like that."

"Is plenty a we Jamaicans have we roots on the plantation them, you know," Miss Mildred commented.

"I know, but when Grampy used to tell me 'bout when him people was living on the plantation and working for the white people, Grammy Iris would tell him not to fill up my head with all them stories because I must move on to bigger and better things.

"Your grandma right. What you say she name?"

"Iris. I get my middle name from her and my first name from Grampy's mother. He tell them to call me Elizabeth, just like him mother."

"Then you have a special name so you mus' hear what you grandmother say. You cut out for bigger and better things. So you know what that mean…jus' make up your mind and talk to Miss Cynthia about your schooling. I will back you up if you need me. But just do it. Alright?"

Beth nodded and smiled broadly.

Two weeks later Beth was a newly enrolled student in Mrs. James's private school for young ladies. To her surprise and joy Mrs. Henley had agreed to allow her two evenings off per week to attend classes. Mrs. James, too, had been very accommodating, accepting Beth's proposal to wash clothes in exchange for tutelage. Beth liked Mrs. James. She was an Englishwoman who had come to Jamaica over thirty years ago to teach. She had decided to settle down on the island even after retirement. Now she had her own school and was known for allowing even the penniless to attend classes.

Even Mr. Henley had been supportive of Beth. He sometimes entertained the girls on Sunday afternoons while she studied and had even helped her a few times with her sums. Beth could not believe her good fortune. She had a new respect for the Henleys. Once, the cook had questioned her about the man's interest in her work but she just shrugged it off. Mildred could hardly read and could never be expected to understand the discussions of educated folk, she thought.

Beth settled into her new life in Kingston, grateful for the opportunity to fulfil her dream. She knew if she were still back home there would be little chance that she would be preparing for the Senior Cambridge Examinations. She still missed her family immensely, especially her father, but she resigned herself to her new life and dedicated all her free time to her studies. She was determined to show everyone in Bonny Gate, but especially her mother, that she could make it without them.

All went well for Beth until one night she woke up, shivering hard. She called out to Mildred who was the closest substitute for the mother she wished was with her right now. When the woman put her hand on her forehead it was burning with fever. Mildred quickly washed Beth's body with Bay Rum, wrapped her tightly in a sheet then left her in bed to sweat out the fever. By morning it was gone but she still felt weak and her head throbbed.

"Is the water you were playing in last night, you know." This was Mildred's explanation for Beth's sudden illness. "My mother always used to tell me that when rain dewing you must come in or else you goin' catch draught, and is the said thing happen to you."

It was Sunday morning and Mildred was rushing around, getting ready for church. As usual, she was going to be singing on the choir. She usually headed out long before the Henley family although they worshipped at the same church. She was never late. She gave Beth one last check, left a pitcher of orange juice on the nightstand, and departed.

Later, as Beth lay in the narrow bed, the silence of the empty house filled her with loneliness. She wondered at her low spirits – she was usually a very positive person, even when she had problems. Maybe it was because she had never been all alone in this house before. The laughter and screams of the girls had been replaced with uncharacteristic quiet. She felt more alone than she had felt even when she had been put on the bus to Kingston two months ago. She sighed and closed her eyes, willing herself back to sleep.

She had fallen into a light doze when she woke to a heaviness on her forehead. Someone had rested a soft, warm hand there.

"Miss Mildred," she groaned, "how you come back so quick?"

She slowly opened her eyes to a round, white face with a bushy moustache. Beth's eyes flew open wide. "Mr. Henley? What you doing here, sah? Me think you gone to church."

With a smile Mr. Henley removed his hand and stood looking at her. "Yes, I went, but I had to come back to deal with some urgent business. And since Mildred said you were sick I just stopped by to check on you."

"Urgent business, sah? Here at the house?" Beth struggled to sit up, concerned. "Something wrong? What happen?"

"Relax, my dear, don't get so worked up." Mr. Henley gently pushed her back onto the pillow. "It was just, aah, some minor thing I had to handle. Nothing for you to worry about." He smiled warmly then sat down on the stool by her bed. "The question is, how are you feeling?"

"I alright, sah. I just need some rest." She sighed, relieved. "By the time Miss Mildred come from church I will be able to help her with the dinner."

"Silly girl. Do you think I am worried about dinner? I'm concerned about you."

Beth peered up at him, puzzled, but simply said, "Thank you, sah."

Mr. Henley pulled the stool closer to the bed and leaned towards her. "So, you're feeling alright now?" Then his voice became softer as he breathed, "I bet a little massage would work wonders for you."

With that he stretched out a hand to her left shoulder and began to squeeze gently. Beth lay still for a moment, confused. Then, suddenly coming to her senses, she shrugged away and slid lower into the sheets. "Th...thanks, Mr. Henley, but I alright now. You better go back to church before service finish."

Seeing her nervousness he sat back, still smiling. "Don't be shy, girl. How old are you now?"

"Fourteen, sah."

"Fourteen, huh? Big girl, now." He winked at her and then, without warning, leaned forward to press soft lips on her forehead.

Beth jumped, and clutched the thin sheet to her chest. "Mr. Henley! What you doing?"

"Come on, girl," he whispered into her ear, "I know you little black girls know about these things from early. Let me taste a little of that chocolate sweetness."

Beth sucked her breath in sharply, her heart beating hard. She shifted away, trying to slide out the other side of the bed, but he was too quick for her. He grabbed her, halting her flight, and pulled her tightly against his chest.

"Mr. Henley," she panted, "don't do this, sah. I can't do them kind of things."

"Beth, I can make things better for you." He clutched her struggling body close to his own, his grip firm. "Do you want money? You may have it. Just make me feel good, Beth."

"Let me go!" Beth screamed and fought desperately to free herself. In the struggle her elbow caught him on the cheekbone. His head flew back and he fell off the stool, hitting the floor hard.

"You bitch," he shouted, clutching his jaw, "you think you are too good for me?" His voice trembled as he spoke. "Prettier girls than you have worked in this house before and they had no problem giving me what I want." He struggled to his feet and stood glaring at Beth as she cowered in the bed. "You'd better be nice to me. I can make your life miserable in this house." He kicked the stool hard then stomped out of the room, slamming the door shut behind him.

Beth stayed in her room for the rest of the day, feigning illness even to Mildred. The cook seemed perturbed that her home remedies had not worked but Beth assured her that all she needed was a little more rest. Mildred seemed relieved and told her to get all the rest she needed. She served dinner to the family then brought Beth a bowl of chicken soup.

"When you cook this soup, Miss Mildred?" Beth looked up at her in surprise when she walked in with the tray. "I didn't want to give you more work."

"Don't worry about it, me dear. Soup don't take any time to cook. You just eat up and get better fast. Das all I want." Mildred smiled as she rested the tray on her lap.

Beth smiled back in thanks and took a sip of the steaming soup. As the first hot spoonful slid down her throat her stomach growled. She had not realized until now how hungry she was. She felt her head begin to clear as the food revived her. She looked up at the plump woman who looked down at her. "Miss Mildred…" she started to say, then hesitated.

"Yes, me dear?"

"Miss Henley…she vex with me for not serving dinner?"

"Vex? Of course she not vex. She know you sick, child. Why she would be vex?"

Beth did not answer, hiding her nervousness by taking a few more sips of the soup as Mildred watched. Finally, she spoke again, "And what about Mr. Henley? Him not vex?"

"Lawd, pickney, how you worry so much?" Mildred shook her head in exasperation and put her hands on her hips. "Don't let me hear any more worrisome questions out of you. Nobody is vex with you. You are a human being, and you can get sick, just like anybody else. The only somebody vex right now is Mr. Henley, and is not with you. Him probably vex with himself. Him say him bump into the vestry door at church. Him jaw red, you see? But that soon clear up. Is not nothing to worry about. Is jus' that the bruise show up bright on him because him so white."

Mildred straightened the sheets around Beth then turned towards the door. "Now eat up, then catch another nap", she said, and slipped out the door.

Next day Beth felt so guilty about leaving all the work on Miss Mildred that she decided not to pretend illness any longer. She would just try to avoid being in Mr. Henley's presence. She prayed he would not tell his wife what had happened. She knew that if he did, she would be the one placed in the wrong. Somehow, though, she felt he would make no mention of the incident. How would he explain his presence at the house when he should have been at church? She took comfort in that thought. She spent the entire day sticking close to

Mildred then ran back to her room as soon as she got the chance.

Beth did not see Mr. Henley all that morning. She spent the day with Mildred and the girls, boiling coconut drops and baking sweet potato pudding in a coal stove out in the backyard. The girls were excited at being allowed to do "big people" things and so were on their best behaviour all day. Because they were so good the cook selected four of the biggest coconut drops from the pile and they all sat under the Otaheiti apple tree out back and munched the sweet cakes. In the relaxed atmosphere Beth began to feel like her normal self again.

Mr. Henley returned that evening and the tension coiled tightly in her stomach. At six o'clock sharp Mildred rested the heavy tray into her arms and sent her to the dining room to serve dinner. She had to approach Mr. Henley in order to set the tray at the head of the table. Her hands trembled so badly that the china bowls clattered. She put the tray down but moved back too quickly and the bowl of gravy spilled over into the silver tray.

"What is wrong with you, girl? You are so clumsy! Take the tray away and clean up that mess." Mrs. Henley's face was flushed with anger. Beth picked up the tray again and, without looking back, hurried from the room with Mrs. Henley's voice ringing in her ears. "These young girls have so much foolishness in their heads they can't even do their work."

Tearfully, Beth took the tray back to the kitchen where Mildred took it from her, a look of concern on her face. "You feeling alright, honey? You not been yourself since Sunday." Beth could only shake her head as Mildred continued, "You must be still suffering from the effects of the fever. Go to your room and lie down. I will serve the dinner."

Beth needed no further encouragement. With a quick thank you she headed for her room. As she lay on the bed staring up at the ceiling she remembered her fear as she struggled in the strong grasp of the heavy-set man. She was no fool. She had heard about men like him. She shuddered at the memory of his lips on her. What could she do? Who would believe her? It would be her word against those of a well-respected man. She was so afraid Mrs. Henley would never believe her and even if she told Mildred, what good would that do? No matter how nice and motherly the older woman was, she was still just an employee. She had no power over Mr. Henley. In fact, Beth suspected that if Mildred were to get involved Mr. Henley would have no qualms in firing her. She could never do that to her friend.

She threw her arm over her eyes as another thought came to her. What if she gave in? Would things really be better for her? Mr. Henley had promised her money, after all, and it was not as if her family cared. As far as she was concerned they had abandoned her and this was her opportunity to get a lot of money and go back to Bonny Gate in fancy clothes, maybe even in a hired car, and show them how much better she had done than they would ever have imagined. Hadn't Grandma Iris told her she was cut out for bigger and better things? But then, she thought, would Grandma really be proud of her for making it in that way?

She groaned aloud and rolled over onto her side. As she repositioned her head on the pillow her eyes fell on the lone goldfish in the small bowl on top of the chest of drawers. The fish had been a gift from Mrs. James and he was her second best friend, next to Mildred. She thought of how proud she had been when the elderly woman had praised her for outstanding performance and presented her with her new pet. Mrs. James had expressed surprise at how quickly she had caught up with the rest of the class and Beth had felt like she would burst with pride when she had been singled out to lead the reading group. She got up from the bed and went over to the fish bowl, a tight smile curling her lips as she sprinkled cracker crumbs into the water.

For the next few weeks the time passed uneventfully for Beth. She made it her duty to stay out of Mr. Henley's way and threw herself into her school work. Once or twice she caught Mrs. Henley staring hard at her but then the moment passed and she wondered if it was all in her mind.

Soon, the Easter holidays were upon them. Mrs. Henley announced that she was taking the girls and going to Mandeville to visit her sister for the holidays. After they left, the house was quiet with only Mildred, Beth and Mr. Henley. He had not made any further advances and Beth began to feel less threatened. She hoped he had put the incident behind him. The days without Mrs. Henley and the girls were like a holiday for Beth. At last she could lie in bed late, reading or just enjoying the sound of the birds outside her window. She could actually take a nap in the afternoon if she wanted to. There were no children to run after, to dress, to entertain or to nurse. She was enjoying this.

However, things took a turn when Mildred was suddenly called home to Portland. Her father had had a stroke. Beth watched in dismay as Mildred walked down the narrow walkway to the gate then turned to wave goodbye. She wondered if she had made a mistake by not taking the cook into her confidence and asking for help. She had wanted to, but she had seen the distress on Mildred's face when she got the news about her father and had known then that she would have to bear her own burden, at least for a while longer. She could only take comfort in the fact that Mr. Henley had avoided her since the incident. She planned to stay in her room and not come out unless absolutely necessary. As Mildred walked away, Beth turned and went straight to her room. She took out her math text and willed herself to concentrate.

"Beth, what are you making for dinner?"

Beth hissed through her teeth as the sound of the man's voice came through her door. She had been in the bedroom for almost two hours but it was now after five o'clock and she knew that she could not stay inside forever. Luckily, lots of food was left over from the meal from the day before and all she would need to do was reheat the meat and rice. She would then prepare the salad fresh.

She opened the door slowly and peeked out. Mr. Henley was nowhere in sight. She exited the room and walked softly to the kitchen, feeling like a thief in the house. She went about her task hurriedly, hoping not to have to see the man before she got the chance to scurry back to her room. She was almost done when the door to the kitchen opened and he walked in.

"Why have you been avoiding me?"

He leaned against the counter by the door and stared at her. Beth made no reply. Her hands moved quickly as she cut the tomatoes into thin slices.

"Don't you hear me talking to you?" There was annoyance in his voice. He straightened and glared at her.

"You don't have to act so high and mighty, you know. You're just a little black girl like the rest of them. There's no need for airs."

Beth glanced quickly at him then ducked her head and focused again on the bowl of vegetables in front of her – fresh, green lettuce, blood-red tomatoes, cool, white cucumbers. She snipped and sliced with intensity, all the while willing him to go away.

The hawk stood there, silent, watching her. A snake coiled in her stomach.

Then his mood changed. A smile crept across his lips and he spoke gently. "I know what the problem is. You're nervous. Don't worry about it, Beth. Nobody has to know. Let's just have our own little fun."

He cocked his head to one side as he watched her. The snake wound itself tighter. "You make me feel good and I make you feel good. You know I have money, and that's all you need, isn't it?" The voice was sickly sweet syrup – taunting, repulsing. "You could get anything you want. I'd make sure of it. Just share some pleasure with me and we'll both be happy. So…what about it?"

As he spoke he moved closer…and closer still. The snake coiled tight, tight in her belly, twisting her insides till she almost buckled over in pain. The man lifted his hand to touch her and she spun around, teeth bared, the knife pointing straight at his chest.

"If you touch me I sink this knife right in you belly." She spoke through clenched teeth, fighting to keep the snake inside. Her chest heaved with the rising urge to strike. "I prepare to go to prison before I let you put your nasty hands on me."

Mr. Henley stopped in his tracks, eyes wide. But Beth did not stop. She could not. All the fear and anger that had been festering inside her boiled over.

"Yes! Me is a little black girl - no money, no nothing. But me is a girl you not goin' to get today! White man rape my great-grandmother but it not goin' happen to me. In case you never hear, slavery done!"

The man stared wildly at her and backed away quickly. "I… I'm sorry, Beth. I didn't mean anything by this. P...please…"

Beth raised the knife high above her head and the man shrank away, wild terror in his eyes. He watched her raised hand in fascination, the hot thrill of the hunt gone, leaving nothing but cold fear. The hawk disintegrated before her eyes. He was nothing…nothing but a pile of fluff.

With a look of disgust Beth threw the knife into the sink. She turned her back on the cowering man and strode towards the living room. At the front door she stopped then turned.

"I not staying here with you, you sick dog," she shouted, her voice dripping with contempt for him. "This is one black girl you not goin' to get pregnant in this house. I leaving here for good!"

With that she flung the front door open and stared straight into the shocked face of Mrs. Henley. She was at the doorway, suitcase in hand, her daughters standing wide-eyed behind her.

Without a word Beth marched past them and never looked back.

Chapter 4

1969

"Miss Pauline!" Leonie called as she leaned against the doorbell, her arms full of bags. "Pauline, open up!"

It was already five-twenty and she was rushing to get to a six o'clock staff meeting in Ocho Rios. She had just enough time to stop at the house to drop off the groceries so that the nanny could prepare dinner for the children.

"Pau…" As Leonie opened her mouth to call again the door opened and the elderly woman greeted her.

"Lord, Miss Leonie. How you weigh down yourself so with the bags. Mind you strain yourself, you know."

"It's alright, Miss P. Just help me with these." She handed a couple of the bags to the woman then struggled down the hallway to the kitchen where she dumped the rest of them on the table. "Where are the children?"

"Lionel in him room doing homework and Princess in her bed. She don't wake up yet."

"Really? She fell asleep late?"

"She didn't go into that bed until about five o'clock. Just romping, romping all day. So you know she won't be up for another hour or so."

"Don't let her sleep past six-thirty or I will have hell to get her to bed tonight. Anyway, I have to head back for the staff meeting so just put these away for me and make sure Lionel is in bed by nine, okay." She headed for her son's bedroom and peeked in. He was sitting on the floor, pushing a red and blue train back and forth.

"Hello, Lionel," Leonie whispered. He looked up with a start then smiled broadly at her.

"Mama! What you doin' here? Miss Pauline said you coming home late tonight."

"Well," she smiled as she went over to kneel on the floor beside him, "I have to go back to school for a staff meeting, so she was right. I'll be home late. I just dropped off the groceries but I'll have to get going in a few minutes."

"Aaw, Mama. You always goin' to staff meetings."

"Come on, Lionel," Leonie soothed. "They're only once a month. And you always love it when I bring goodies home from the meeting."

"Oh, yeah." His pout was replaced with a smile. His small, white teeth were like pieces of chalk against the blackboard of his handsome face. Leonie marvelled at how much he was beginning to look like his father, even at eleven years of age.

"So where is this homework I hear you were doing? I don't see any books."

"Cho, it too boring. I just taking a break."

"Now, now, Lionel…"she began, but he cut her off.

"I know, I know. I can't become a doctor if I don't do my homework."

"Yes, so get cracking, hear me?" She leaned over and kissed his forehead then got up and headed for the door.

"Hey. I just remembered something." She turned and smiled broadly. "I have something special for you."

"You got me another train?"

"No, something for your collection."

With a gasp, Lionel jumped up. "Did you get it?"

"I got it." Leonie grinned and pulled a crisp bank-note from her pocket and held it up between both index fingers and thumbs for her son to see. "The new Jamaica Dollar. One of the first set issued by the Treasury."

"Wow," Lionel held out his hand and took it gently from his mother's fingers. "This goin' to look so good in my album."

"It's beautiful, isn't it? No more pounds and shillings for us, Lionel. Jamaica's all grown up now."

"Like you?"

"Something like that." She grinned again, and ruffled his hair. "Anyway, I've got to go. See you later."

After she had pulled the door shut behind her she made a quick stop in Princess's room where she stroked the child's forehead for just a few seconds and kissed a soft cheek.

As Leonie drove the six miles to Ocho Rios her thoughts were on her family. She was proud of Lionel who would be starting high school in September. Princess would be entering the local infant school. She was finally beginning to have some stability and order in her life.

Her early years at the University of the West Indies had been rough. Her mother had been her only source of support and money had often run short. When she finally found a part-time job on campus it eased the pressure to a great extent.

While in her third year at the university Leonie met and fell in love with Raphael Ramjeet. She loved his free-thinking spirit and radical views. She also loved his sense of adventure and his brilliant humour and wit. But most of all she loved his zest for life. He seemed to enjoy everything he did. He studied with zeal, he played hard and he ate as if every meal were his last. He savoured every bite and even licked his fingers in public. He ate practically everything and anything, but especially if it had been curried. After just two months with him Leonie had learnt to prepare curried chicken, curried mutton, curried beef, curried vegetables and she was even prepared to curry his desserts if he wished. Thankfully, he never asked.

In 1957, after knowing each other for only nine months, they got married. A year later, Lionel was born. The couple enjoyed a happy marriage for about six years - until his mother moved in. Mrs. Ramjeet and her son looked nothing like each other. While Raphael was thin and dark, she was a fat, light-skinned Indian woman who was as old fashioned and conservative as they came. She could not fathom why her son, a full-blooded Indian, had chosen to marry a black girl. There were so many young Indian girls from their village who would have loved to catch this university-educated man. There were not that many Indian men in Jamaica, anyway, so the ones who were available were pursued aggressively. But while the Indian girls of Old Harbour awaited his return Raphael did the unforgivable - he crossed racial lines and chose a black woman instead.

Mrs. Ramjeet was beside herself with anger. She could not bring herself to be on friendly terms with Leonie - she did not even try. Leonie's distress could not have been greater when Raphael told her that he wanted his mother to come and live with them.

Despite her protests her mother-in-law was moved in. It was then that Leonie realized how much influence the woman had over her son. On campus Raphael had been his own man, defending radical views and leading groups of students in protests but at home with his mother he was a little boy again. It was as if he were afraid to contradict her on anything. He never even told Leonie why he had decided to move her into the house. It was not until six weeks after the move, when she received a phone call from the doctor, that she realized that Mrs. Ramjeet was dying from cancer.

The situation got worse when medical bills began to pile up and they began to run into debt. Mrs. Ramjeet's health deteriorated rapidly and it demanded a constant supply of medication to help her fight the pain. The rounds of chemotherapy were scheduled but they did not seem to help. As his mother moved closer to death Raphael grew more distant. Eventually, he stopped coming home for dinner.

Instead, he started drinking. With the drinking came the quarrels and fights and then the beatings.

Mid-thought, Leonie suddenly remembered that she was low on gas. What she had in the car would definitely not take her as far as Ocho Rios. Seeing a Shell gas station a little distance away she headed towards it and pulled in. As the attendant pumped the gas her mind raced back five years…

Whack! The heavy palm connected with Leonie's jaw with full force. Her head snapped back and she staggered backwards, crashing into the wall.

"Mama!" Lionel's scream pierced the sudden blackness that threatened to envelop her. He ran to her and threw his chubby arms around her head.

"Mama," he sobbed.

"Get back to your room. Now!" Lionel shrank away

from his father but still clung desperately to his mother's arms. Leonie shook her head and moaned as her eyes slowly began to clear. She heard Lionel wailing loudly by her side and raised her eyes to see her husband standing over them, hands on his hips, glaring. Raphael took a menacing step towards them and Lionel shrieked and ran from the room.

Suddenly, he stopped. It was as if his son's scream hit a nerve. He looked down at his wife then shook his head as if in confusion. With a growl deep in his throat he turned and stomped out of the room.

Leonie slowly pulled herself up from the ground and leaned against the chest of drawers by the closet. There was a humming sound in her ears and her eyes were brimming with tears. This was just another in the many episodes that she had to endure with her abusive husband. It did not take much to trigger his anger. This time it was because she had 'disrepected' him by not opening the front door fast enough when he knocked.

According to Raphael he had forgotten his house keys and had been knocking for quite a while before she finally came to let him in. All she remembered was waking from a deep sleep to the knocks, pulling on her robe and heading for the front door.

As soon as he entered he started shouting at her. She realized that he was terribly drunk and tried to calm him down but it was to no avail. Eventually the shouting woke Lionel who came out of his bedroom, crying. Despite the presence of his son Raphael's sneers got even uglier.

"Where you been? I been out there twen'y minutes knocking. Where the hell you been?" His voice was slurred and spittle flew from his mouth as he spoke.

"Raphael…I was asleep."

"Asleep? You expect me to believe that? You knew I was out there. You think I'm a fool?"

"But I came as soon as I heard the knocking."

"Shut up, you lying…I bet you wanted to teach me a lesson, eh?"

"No, Raphael…"

"I said shut up! I don't want another word coming out of your lying mouth. Getting all high and mighty, eh? Think you're too good for me now, eh?" With every word he took a step closer and Leonie backed away. She could see Lionel standing at the door, wide eyed and trembling.

"Raphael, stop this. Please!" Leonie pulled the robe tightly around her and walked quickly back to the bedroom. She tried to push the door shut behind her but he was right on her heels. He stuck his foot in the door and shoved with such force that he slammed her back against the wall.

"Where you think you're going? I'm talking to you."

"Raphael," Leonie pleaded, but he was beyond reasoning.

"Where is the respect?" His voice was slurred but his anger was palpable. "You know what they've been saying on the streets? That 'him woman haffi mind him'. You been spreading all kind of scandal about me!"

"Raphael, what are you talking about?"

"You know what I am talking about! Ever since I lost my job at the ministry I know you've been lauding it over me and telling people how you have to cover the expenses. You think I don't know?"

"I have never discussed our finances with anybody! What do you think I am?"

"You're a liar…" he swayed then grabbed the door jamb for support, "…a liar and a slut, that's what you are."

Leonie gasped as if she had been punched in the stomach. She stared at her husband and whispered, "How could you? I've been faithful to you from the day we met and you dare say something as cruel as that?"

"You're jus' like any other woman. As soon as a man down you…you take full advantage. So is who now, eh? That teacher guy who dropped Lionel home last week? Or that insurance agent I walked in on two days ago?"

"I don't have to listen to this. You've gone mad!" And with that, Leonie pushed as if to go past him. And that's when it happened.

"Don't walk away when I'm talking to you!" He grabbed her arm and dragged her backwards. She struggled against him and tried to push forward. With a growl of anger he pushed her backwards then raised his hand and slapped her full on the jaw. As Leonie fell she heard Lionel's scream ringing in her ears.

Six weeks later Leonie sat staring in shock at Doctor Robinson's face. "What do you mean, pregnant?" Her heart thumped hard in her chest and she prayed it was all a dream.

With a broad smile on his dark round face the man said, "Yes, Mrs. Ramjeet, you're pregnant. You'll have an addition to the family in approximately seven months. Congratulations."

"Pregnant." Leonie's voice left her in a whisper. This was just about the worst thing that could happen to her right now. She had only missed one period but she had thought it was due to stress. Now her worst fear had come true.

"Th…thank you, doctor." She smiled weakly as she rose and picked up her handbag.

As Leonie drove her mind raced. She had been holding on to a traumatic marriage for the sake of her son and now there would be another complication in her life. She just could not deal with it. She had avoided Raphael's rare advances until the night he had overpowered her. As she surrendered to his manhandling she prayed that the incident would pass and simply be a bad memory but she knew now that it would be much more than that. It would lead to another person becoming a part of her life. She could not let that happen.

"Oh, God," she breathed, tears trickling down her cheeks as she drove. "Why this? Why now?" She had suffered at Raphael's hands but, because of her son, she had endured it all. She knew he needed his father so she suffered humiliation, indignation, and abuse for his sake. It was not for her, it was never for her. She loved her son and would do anything to make things right for him.

Raphael knew this and he took full advantage of the situation. He played on her love for Lionel and even taunted her about how she would sacrifice anything for the child. But Leonie knew she could not bring another one into the world right now. There was just too much going on in her life, things she could not manage, things that were overwhelming her. Right now all she had energy for was herself and her son, nobody else. She was going to end this before it even started. That was the only way out.

Her mind made up, Leonie wiped the tears away with the back of her hand. There was no alternative. And, of course, Raphael would never know.

That weekend Leonie took Lionel for a quick visit to his grandmother's house in Bonny Gate. While he ran off to play with the goats she sat on a low stool in the kitchen and helped Beth peel the potatoes. As usual, her mother was plying her with questions.

"Mama," Leonie shook her head in frustration, "there is nothing wrong with me. Will you stop bugging me?"

The older woman only grunted as she stood in front of the stove, stir-frying onions and green peppers in a skillet.

"You come from right out of this womb here. Not because you big. You are my daughter and I know you. I know something wrong."

"So you are a psychic now, Mama?"

"Not psychic - I just know mi pickney."

Leonie smiled ruefully and shook her head. She could never get things past her mother.

The older woman wiped her hands in her apron and sat down heavily in a nearby chair. "I know you going through a lot right now. But you have to be strong for you and your son. And don't sacrifice your life for anybody."

"Mama, you know it is only because of Lionel that I stay. He needs his father. If I have to sacrifice my life for anybody it would be for Lionel. He's my son!"

"You think when Lionel grow big him going to thank you for sitting in this and suffering like a dog for his sake. Do better than that, Leonie. I never raise you like this." Beth's voice was sharp.

"What you mean, Mama? I don't like where this is going, you know." She dropped both potato and knife into the pan and stared at her mother's stern face.

"You don't like when I talk about this because I don't mash my words. Leonie, you can't make somebody strong unless you make yourself strong first. What you think you teaching the child when you sit down and let a man batter-bruise you so, in front of him. You think you teaching him to be a man?"

"But Raphael never hit Lionel. You know he loves his son. How can I take Lionel from him? And Lionel would miss his father!"

"Yes, hide behind that. When your son grow up to be a man and start to slap women all over the place don't question where he get that from. I tell you before and I will tell you again. You hurting the child more than you helping him. You are my daughter but you know I have to speak me mind. I'm not into this pussy-footin' round the truth. You weak, Leonie. All you teaching your son is how to be a victim."

"Mama, you can say anything. You never had to go through what I'm going through now, so don't tell me I'm weak. I'm making choices for the sake of my son and if you can't deal with it, well so be it. Until Lionel is old enough I will stay with his father and I will make sure that they have a good relationship because I think that is the best thing for him." Leonie picked up the large knife and began to peel again. "When he is old enough I will leave."

"And when will that be?" Leonie did not reply but kept on slicing the potato, her eyebrows knitted as if in deep concentration. Beth grunted and continued, "Next thing you know another one will be on the way and then you have to wait on that one to grow up, too. You know, I can see that you working hard to never leave that man."

Leonie blinked rapidly as tears stung her eyes. The rest of her mother's words were lost as she felt her heart sink.

Without looking at the older woman she rose and picked up her handbag. "Mama, go get Lionel. I'm ready to leave now."

It was days before Leonie could think of the conversation with her mother without feeling pain. As she packed up her books from her last class her thoughts went back to the conversation and she shook her head in frustration. Her mother would never understand. It was not that she wanted to continue suffering but she wanted what was best for her son. And then there was that little complication of still loving Raphael.

With a sigh she threw her bag over her shoulder and walked to the door. Suddenly a little boy of about nine or ten years ran up to her and said, "Miss, the principal say you must come to him office right now."

"Now? But I'm getting ready to leave."

"Him say you must come now, Miss."

Leonie rolled her eyes without letting the little boy see and turned towards the staff room. If this was another assignment at this time of the day she would have to put her foot down and just let Mr. Robertson know that she had a family. This was not the first time he had done this. She knew it would not be the last but she would certainly let her displeasure be known. As she entered the staff room there was a slight frown on her face.

"Yes, Mr. Robertson? You caught me just heading out the door."

"Mrs. Ramjeet, I'm glad I caught you." As he spoke he rose from behind the desk and came towards her. She took a step back in surprise as he caught her hand. "You must go to the hospital right now."

"Wh…why?"

"There has been an accident. Your husband and son have been rushed to the Saint Ann's Bay Hospital. You must go to them right now."

"Oh, my God," she gasped, "oh, my God!"

"Calm down, Mrs. Ramjeet. Just stay calm. I've already called a taxi for you. I don't think you should be driving in this state. It will be here in another minute so just hold on." As Leonie staggered against him Mr. Robertson pulled her gently over to a chair and set her down. No sounds came. There were no tears. She just stared, not seeing, her heart pounding and her thoughts racing wildly. Lionel! What if anything happened to Lionel? And Raphael? She prayed desperately that they were alright.

By the time the taxi dropped her off at the emergency ward she was a mess of nerves. She could hardly control her trembling as she spoke to the nurse at the registration desk, praying silently that she would not have to face even worse news.

The situation was grave. Lionel had been brought to the emergency room unconscious, and still was. They had already done X-rays and found that he had three broken ribs and some internal bleeding. He had also sustained head injuries. In the accident he had been thrown through the windshield. He was lucky to be alive, but there was still a possibility that he might not survive. The doctors promised to do their best but at this point, they said, it was in the hands of God.

Raphael, on the other hand, had escaped with just a bump on the forehead. He would not have to spend even one night in the hospital. As she sat by her son's bedside staring at the still, almost lifeless figure, she raised tear-filled eyes to her husband who stood by her side.

"What happened?"

"I…I don't even know for sure." Raphael looked away from her and rubbed his chin. "The dog came out of nowhere. I…I just swerved to avoid him and the next thing I knew, I was running off the road."

Leonie glared at him. "You almost killed my son for the sake of a dog?"

"It was an accident!" Raphael raked his fingers through his hair and turned to look out the window. With his back still turned to her he said softly, "And he's my son, too."

As she listened to his whining voice she suddenly felt a strong dislike for the subdued man who stood in front of her.

But it was not until the police came later that day that she knew she hated him. There had been no dog. Raphael had been speeding. And at three o'clock in the afternoon, even while knowing that it was his turn to drive their son home from school, he had been drinking.

The days Leonie spent by Lionel's bed, watching him slowly recover, were days of pain, relief and realization. Her son almost had to lose his life for her to realize that she had been placing him in danger all along. She could have lost him just like that, simply because she was too spineless to stand up to a man who abused her, frightened his own child, and was too irresponsible to put his son's well-being before his own pleasure.

She knew what she had to do. She, her son, and the child just beginning to form inside her, would survive…without Raphael Ramjeet.

"That's it, Mam?" The voice of the gas station attendant broke into Leonie's reverie. "Don't need to top up the oil or nothing?"

"No, thank you." Leonie blinked then smiled as she handed him the money. "Keep the change."

"Thanks, Mam." The young man's face brightened at the sight of the bills. "Have a good evening."

With a nod, Leonie drove out of the gas station and onto the main road. She was going to have a good evening, alright. It had been five years since she had made that momentous decision and she did not regret it. She had come a long way and she had a long way to go still, but she was her own woman and she was never turning back.

Chapter 5

1974

"Let me in!"

It was Princess, as usual, bugging the heck out of him. She was the most annoying nine-year-old Lionel knew. He hissed through his teeth as she pounded on his bedroom door.

"Let me in, Lionel!"

"Leave me alone, pest!"

He hated it when his mother made him babysit Princess.

She had decided to go to the supermarket after work so he was stuck walking Princess home from school – and he ended up missing the football match between Santos and Wadadah. He had been waiting for weeks to see the Kingston boys get a good whipping from his favourite team. Now he would only be able to hear about it from his friends. He could have wrung Princess's neck.

He was supposed to make sure she did her homework before his mother got home but as soon as they went into the house and he saw his sister pull her books out of her school bag he considered his work done. He wanted to be left alone. Who wanted to spend the evening with a nagging girl pickney, anyway?

When the banging did not stop he threw himself off the bed and flung the door open. Princess stood there, glaring up at him.

"Why you don't go find something do?" he growled.

"You're supposed to be heating up my dinner. You know Mummy doesn't like me messing with the stove." She folded her arms across her chest and planted herself squarely in the doorway.

"Look. I'm doing my work," he snapped. When she did not move he pushed her roughly aside and stalked off towards the kitchen. "Come feed your hungry belly and then stop bugging me!"

Princess followed him down the hallway then veered right towards the living room.

"So where you going?" Lionel turned and shouted at her retreating back. "You not coming to help me?"

"For what? You're the one who is supposed to be taking care of me, remember?"

"Yeah, I remember," he muttered, "but I soon get the hell out of here."

He opened the refrigerator and pulled out two saucepans. Within minutes the aroma of brown stewed chicken filled the house. He scooped rice onto a plate then smothered it with the chicken stew, just the way Princess liked it.

He headed for the dining room where he plopped the plate on the table.

"Come get your dinner," he yelled, "but you can go get your own lemonade. You don't have no slave in here."

He did not even wait for Princess to come to the table. He grabbed his own plate and a fork and headed back to his room. He kicked the door shut behind him and flopped down on the bed. Then he kicked his Spanish book to the floor.

"Who the heck am I going to talk Spanish to, anyway," he mumbled as he chewed a mouthful of the savoury stew. He had only put the book on the bed in case his mother came home early and peeked in to see if he was studying. He had promised her that he would and he just wanted to make the lie convincing.

But he had no interest in the Spanish language. In fact, outside of music, there was no subject in which he had any special interest. So, instead of studying, he spent most of his time listening to music. Practically all of his pocket money was spent on forty-fives and eight tracks. He owned every album the Wailers had produced. The group had recently broken up but Lionel was ecstatic when the new group, Bob Marley and the Wailers, was formed. When it came to Bob Marley's music he just could not get enough.

When Lionel was not listening to Reggae or hanging out with his friends he did just enough studying to pass his classes. And this was only because his mother kept nagging.

His teacher had called her in, complaining that his grades had fallen. They even questioned whether he was to be allowed to take the General Certificate Exams. His mother had pleaded with the principal because this was his last year - he was in fifth form.

He had sat in stony silence as she argued that, without his GCE's, there was no way he would get into university. She explained that she had done all she could to provide the best education for him. She had even paid for him to do private lessons during the past year. Little did she know what a waste that was, he thought wryly. He had hardly shown up for his lessons and the tutor never said a word. He just collected his money faithfully at the end of each month.

Lionel did not care much for going to university. In fact, he would much rather find a job right after high school. He would be out of school in the next seven months and then he would be free. He was dying to get out of the house, to be on his own, to be a real man.

The problem was, his mother loved him too much. But instead of making him happy her love only annoyed him. She mothered him and pampered him to the point where some of his friends called him 'Mama's Boy'. He hated it.

He even hated the way she babied Princess. And what kind of a dumb name was that, anyway? She looked more like a round dumpling than a princess. Ever since she had come into his life when he was seven years old she had been nothing but a pain. When she was a baby all she ever did was scream, throw up and take all his mother's time and attention. Things would have been so much better if she had never shown up, he thought. His father had left when she was still in his mother's belly and Lionel had always felt that this had something to do with his departure. He hated his sister for that.

As for his father, he hated him too. Just the thought of him made him grit his teeth. He sucked his teeth and threw himself back into the pillows, willing himself to wipe his father from his mind.

Yeah, he thought, he would have to find a job and leave this house - and soon. The main problem was that he did not know if he would get hired. He would have just turned seventeen at graduation and most companies took on workers eighteen years and older. He probably could try out as a mechanic's apprentice, he reasoned. He had heard that mechanics made good money and he had always liked to work with his hands.

He nodded as he made mental plans for his departure. He would work as an apprentice and rent a room somewhere far away from here. Then he would never have to deal with his nagging mother or his whining sister again.

Lionel was smiling as he pulled the drawer of his nightstand open then put a fat spliff between his lips.

"Whe' you a say, rasta! Gi' me five!"

Lionel turned to see Junior's outstretched palms. With a grin he slapped them then asked, "What the programme for today, man?"

"What time your last class finish?"

"Two-thirty, but I can even skip that. Cho, the teacher would not even miss me. Boring social studies." He took the toothpick from between his teeth and flicked it into the bushes. "Who want to know nothing 'bout no stupid bauxite levy, anyway. If the government want tax the foreigner them pon de bauxite that is fi them business. We not getting nothing out of it, anyway, just the politician them."

"Jus' ditch that class, man. Link me at one o'clock behind the woodwork shop. I have a proposal for you."

With a wink Junior sauntered off, whistling as he went.

Later, as Lionel sat in Math class, he thought about what his friend might have in mind. Junior was a really crazy guy, always coming up with wicked ideas, always playing pranks. The last crazy plan Junior had was for them to pretend to be older and to sneak into a go-go club. That had required him sneaking out of the house at eleven o'clock in the night but he had done it. They had gotten into the Romeo Lounge without any problem. Both of them were tall and could pass for eighteen.

The Romeo Lounge was a dingy nightclub on the outskirts of Ocho Rios. It was so dark in there you could hardly see. Smoke wafted through the air and people milled around at the bar. But the boys were not interested in any of this. They headed straight for the dance floor on which there was a platform where three half naked girls danced slowly to the rub-a-dub music. On their way they bumped into people clinging to each other, grinding to the music.

But the go-go dancers were the main attraction for the young men. On a Wednesday night when the dancers did their work topless the place would be packed. The boys found a table close to the platform and sat down to watch.

A waitress came to take their orders. Junior ordered a beer but Lionel passed, too absorbed with the scene to be thirsty. He did not like the taste of beer, anyway. As the girls danced Junior took sips of his beer then he dipped into his pocket and pulled out two spliffs. He passed one to Lionel. Both of them lit up and drew deeply as they watched. No one objected. In a place like this, no one would.

"Mr. Ramjeet!"

Lionel jumped as Mr. Williams pointed the chalk at him.

"To the blackboard, young man. Let's see how much you've retained from today's class."

Lionel's heart pounded. He had not heard a word. He knew it, and the teacher knew it. Well, he would just have to fudge his way through, as usual. Grumbling under his breath, he pushed back his chair and walked slowly to the blackboard amidst giggles from the girls and sniggers from the boys.

His classmates loved the entertainment. They, too, had been bored with the Math class and relished the thought of some distraction. He groaned as he took the piece of chalk from the teacher's hand. He had no idea what he was going to write on the board. This was not going to be pretty.

That afternoon Lionel was still feeling a bit deflated as he walked to the back of the woodwork shop to meet Junior but his mood perked up when his friend asked, "How you would like to make some good money?"

"What kinda question that? Of course, man."

"Look here."

Lionel's eyes bulged as Junior turned out his pocket to reveal a wad of ten dollar bills.

"Where you get so much money?"

"Is for me to know and for you to find out," Junior smirked.

Lionel was bursting with curiosity. "Cho, man, just spill the beans."

"I know a man that can give me nuff weed. One little bag and that's ten whole dollars. You know how much money you can make in a day?"

"You talking 'bout selling drugs? You mad?"

"Cho, man, it easy. And with all dem guy roun' de place a look weed to buy, dem might as well buy it from us. The school full a people who smoke weed. Just like we."

"Bwoy, mi nuh know…me never even think about selling weed before. That illegal, you know."

"So is smoking it. Don't be a wimp. Look how much money me make off it." He thrust the wad of bills under Lionel's nose. "If you do this you won't even have to worry about work after graduation. You set for life!"

"But it dangerous… what if we get in trouble?"

"So who goin'talk? All you have to do is find some special customers who can keep them mouth shut and you just keep them supplied. That's it. You don't need nothing more than that."

"Bwoy, I don't know…if them ever catch me, my mother would kill me…"

"Don't worry, man. You won't get caught. Anyway, is not your mother you should be worrying 'bout. Mothers, them soft. Them will let you off the hook. Is the ole man you mus' worry 'bout. I know mine would bruck me up if him ever find out."

Lionel sucked his teeth. "Ole man? I not even see that man or hear from him since I was twelve. I only know that once in a while him send a cheque to my mother. That's it." His voice was rough with emotion.

It was still painful to talk about his father. He felt he would never get over the pain. Maybe it would be a good thing if he did get caught selling drugs, he thought. Then his father would be sorry he had left. Then again, maybe he would be glad if Lionel were sent to some prison. That would mean one less set of maintenance cheques.

He felt the anger rise in him and unshed tears burned his eyes. He looked at Junior. "Me ready. Give me the details."

As the judge's gavel fell Lionel watched his mother struggle to hold back the tears. He had been involved in selling drugs for four months and the business was going well but it ended when someone reported him to the Form Teacher. The principal called the police.

Caught with several bags of the weed, Lionel could do nothing but confess. Now he was faced with twelve months in Saint James Remedial School. No G.C.E.'s for him now. Graduation was only a month away but he would not be a part of it.

He kept his eyes averted, too ashamed to look his mother in the face. He knew he had hurt her deeply and dared not face her pain.

Without a backward glance he followed the guard out of the room.

Life in remedial school was like torture for Lionel. Back at home he would have had his own room where he could watch television when he liked. He could visit his friends when he liked. In his new home he slept in a bunk bed and shared a dorm room with five other boys. His television time was restricted to specific shows on weekends and, as for friends, he had none.

His mother had come to visit him five times already but each time he had given her a cool reception.

He remained glum. He never heard from his father and was afraid to ask his mother if she had told him what happened. Although her eyes pleaded with him he never had much to say to her. He was too ashamed, too hurt, and too angry with her, with his father, with the world.

Lionel found that his new school was full of angry people. He kept out of the way of the other boys as much as possible. Sometimes, though, no matter how hard he tried, he would end up getting into trouble with them. Some of them just had something to prove. Today was P.E and he felt that, like so many other days, this one was not going to be incident-free.

Lionel was one of the first boys on the football field. The coach was a stickler for time. He meted out severe punishment for lateness. The first time Lionel was late he had to do twenty push-ups plus two laps around the field. He never exercised when he was at home so he was far from fit and was exhausted at the end of that session.

He was going to make sure that this did not happen again. Just being sent to remedial school for a year had given him the biggest scare of his life. He wanted to be able to survive. He did not want to do anything that would lengthen his sentence.

When the coach arrived he immediately placed the boys into two teams and the game began. It was rough going for Lionel who was tall but very thin. His lanky form was no match for the burly youths who threw themselves at the ball and at him. He had been called 'wimpy' and 'girl' by some of the bigger, more aggressive boys.

He soon learned to simply stay out of their way both on the football field and off. But today his efforts would be in vain.

Coach Thomas blew his whistle and the game began. Lionel's team had lost last time and some of the boys had insinuated that it was his fault. This time he was determined to prove himself on the field.

Forty minutes into the game the biggest boy on the field rushed over to tackle the ball from him but Lionel was determined to hold on to it and the encounter soon became a scuffle.

The bigger boy elbowed Lionel and pushed him to the ground. In return, Lionel shot a foot out and brought his aggressor crashing down. With a yell of rage the boy threw himself on top of Lionel and pummelled him with heavy fists. By the time the coach ran up to them, whistle shrieking, several heavy blows had already landed on Lionel's face.

As the coach dragged him off, his opponent snarled, "Watch me and you later. Me a go bus' you up."

Lionel's heart sank. He had tried so hard but now a fight seemed inevitable.

That evening after dinner Lionel sat on his bunk, waiting. Although he was hoping the ruffian had changed his mind he was not to be disappointed. Three rough-looking boys approached his bunk, one of them the boy from the football field.

"Get up. You coming with us," he growled.

"Where?" Lionel's voice sounded a lot stronger than he felt.

"We goin' to the gym. We goin' to settle this thing tonight."

Each of the assistant goons, as Lionel had come to think of them, grasped one of his arms and pulled him up off the bed. They forced him out of the dormitory and along the pathway that led to the building that housed the gym. It was empty and the front door was locked. That did not deter them. They dragged Lionel to the back of the building where the biggest boy proceeded to quickly pick the lock.

When they got inside they walked him briskly to the back of gym towards the boxing ring.

"Boxing?" Lionel pulled away, confused. "You want me to box?"

"Yeah. Get up in that ring."

Then it dawned on him. The boy who had wrestled him to the ground was also a member of the boxing team. He would get murdered in that ring. But he could not back down now. This was virtually a test of his manhood.

Both boys fitted gloves and the fight began.

In less than five minutes Lionel's face was red and battered. The bigger boy rained blows on Lionel's face and stomach. He was no competition for the boxer.

"Stop dat right now. Get outta here before I beat all o' oonu to a pulp."

At the sound of the gruff voice the three bullies turned and stared. When they saw who it was they jumped out of the boxing ring and dashed out of the gym leaving Lionel curled up on the canvas, alone.

Slowly, he struggled to his feet and looked at the person who had spoken. He felt his heart tighten. He was staring into the fierce eyes of the most feared boy in the school –Blacka, the Beast.

"Hey, Coolie bwoy, you don't hear me say you must scatta? Now!"

He shouted the last word at Lionel then walked up to the boxing ring, an ugly sneer on his face. Lionel slowly backed away from the ropes, still clutching his aching belly.

Blacka was at least six feet three inches tall and burly. Although he could not have been more than seventeen years old he already looked like a fully grown man, with Popeye-like arms and a stubbly beard covering his chin.

The other boys said he had been in Saint James since he was fourteen and was not going to be released until his eighteenth birthday. Outside of his immediate gang, boys either gave him a wide berth or scurried to carry out his orders. It would not do to annoy a boy of his size and reputation. No one was quite sure about this but it was also rumoured that he had killed his own sister - with his bare hands.

Lionel's breath caught in his throat as he watched Blacka climb over the ropes and into the boxing ring. Sweat stung his armpits. His breath came in shallow gasps. He knew he stood no chance against this mass of muscle.

Suddenly he blurted, "You goin' do me like your sister?"

The words had flown out of his mouth before he could stop them. What in heaven's name had made him say that? If he wasn't dead meat before, he knew he was now. Sucking in his breath he clenched his eyes shut and steeled himself for the blow.

Seconds passed. Nothing. More seconds. Silence. Lionel's held breath began to strain his lungs. His fear of the blow turned to dread that he would face something even worse. Slowly, he opened his right eye and stared straight into Blacka's grinning face.

"You a idiot, bwoy. You a one o' them fools who believe that story?"

Lionel slowly expelled his breath. He straightened his back and looked up at Blacka in confusion. Laughter? That was the last thing he expected from the Beast.

The big boy laughed out loud as he watched Lionel. "If you evah see you face! How you so stupid, bwoy? You know where that story come from? A me make that up when me jus' come ya."

For a moment Lionel forgot to be scared. He was too curious. "But…why? Why you would say something like that about yourself?" Still clutching his ribs he eased himself slowly back down to the canvas.

"Nuh worry 'bout dat. Me have me reasons." Blacka leaned back against the ropes and looked down at him. Then, to Lionel's surprise, he stretched out a hand to him. "Come. Time fi leave this place."

Blacka's giant hand enclosed Lionel's slim one and he was pulled upright. The bigger boy helped him out of the ring then stuffed his hands into his pockets and sauntered out of the gym, leaving Lionel staring after him.

It was not until a week later that Lionel found out the real reason why the Beast had not walloped him in the boxing ring.

Blacka revealed that Mrs. Ramjeet had been his fifth grade teacher. He remembered seeing Lionel coming to the classroom to see his mother. Mrs. Ramjeet had been one of the few teachers who paid any attention to him. Lionel realized that the only thing that had saved him was Blacka's respect for his mother.

Although he would not have described his new relationship with Blacka as friendship there was some sort of connection between them. They rarely saw each other but when they did they greeted each other in an offhand way. The boys who had beaten him up kept their distance, realizing that there was some level of communication between the two.

Lionel was surprised and a little nervous when one night he got a message to meet Blacka at block eight. He still did not know the other boy very well, at least not enough to be comfortable at the summons. But he knew better than to ignore the instruction. At nine o'clock sharp he was in the empty classroom at block eight.

Blacka walked in alone. The two eyed each other, Lionel with cautiousness, Blacka with apparent confidence. Then Blacka spoke.

"I have something I want you to do for me."

Lionel's caution turned to trepidation. What could he do for a boy like Blacka? He wondered if it had anything to do with drugs. He was afraid to ask.

He wanted no more problems; he just wanted to get out of Saint James. He did not want to stay a moment longer than necessary in this hell of a place.

His voice shook slightly as he spoke. "What you want me to do?"

His nervousness must have been obvious because Blacka chuckled then said, "Just cool, man. Relax yourself. I not asking you to do anything that you can't do."

Then he paused and looked hesitant, seeming almost embarrassed. His voice was low and Lionel could hardly hear his words. "I want you help me with some school work."

Lionel could only stare at him in surprise. Finally, he dragged himself out of his daze. "Sch…school work? I…I thought…" Then, seeing Blacka's scowl he quickly said, "Never mind."

"I need help with my English," Blacka continued. "Me soon haffi leave this place and me no really have no other place to go. The only place me can think of is a little apprenticeship with a mechanic but them tell me that me haffi know English. Them using computers to fix cars now and you haffi know how fi read."

Blacka looked at Lionel, his face serious. "Me need some help with that. Me know that you know the

English stuff. Your mother a teacher so you mus' know them things.

"Sure, I will help you." Lionel nodded vigorously. "No problem, man."

Blacka nodded in acceptance then he paused and stared pointedly at Lionel. "By the way, what a bwoy like you doing in a place like this? How you end up here?"

"Well…" Lionel looked away, the shame still heavy on his heart, "they catch me with some weed…I was goin' sell."

"Wait, the little man is a hustler!" Blacka's broad face broke into a toothy grin. "You certainly don't look it."

"I'm not a hustler," Lionel said sharply, and Blacka raised an eyebrow mockingly. Lionel drew in a breath and continued in a low voice. "I'm not a hustler at all. Is jus'…is jus' the stress get to me, that's all."

"What kind of stress you have so?" Blacka was obviously unconvinced.

"It hard to explain…since my father leave us things just kinda get rough, you know…too much pressure."

"Yeah? Me wouldn't mind if my old man did leave and never come back."

"What you mean?"

"Trust me, if I did stay in that house one more day I woulda murder that man. Him wasn't me real father still, is me stepfather, but him almost try kill me one time. Is only me mother save me." Blacka's mouth twisted in an ugly sneer. "But even she used to smoke ganja and all them something de and drink nuff rum, so is like me never did have no mother anyway." He shook his head slowly. "Trust me, if me did have a teacher mother like yours me know me would go places."

Blacka looked at Lionel with eyes full of sadness but there was a crooked smile on his lips. "You want take my life and give me yours?"

Lionel could swear he saw a glint of a tear in the corner of the boy's left eye. He dropped his eyes and remained silent, not sure how to respond.

The pain in Blacka's eyes touched his heart and he had the sudden realization of how lucky he was to at least have a mother who loved him. Father or no father, he was better off than most of the boys in this school. Blacka was right - what the hell was a boy like him doing in a place like this?

Impulsively, and to Blacka's obvious surprise, Lionel grabbed his arm and said, "Let's go. We have a lot of work to do."

Chapter 6

1980

The bar was crowded. It was Friday night and the beginning of a long weekend. Monday would be National Heroes' Day and the village men and women were looking forward to sleeping in. They would take full advantage of the day off from work, a day without the children running underfoot.

Of course, the children would be made to go to the National Heroes' Day celebrations in the parish capital, Port Maria. Claude Stewart Park would be full of school girls in blue, green and red uniforms and boys in khaki suits. The police would be out in their ceremonial garb and the local bigwigs such as the Mayor and the Members of Parliament would be handing out awards to local heroes.

Tonight, Red Stripe Beer and Guinness Stout flowed freely and men laughed louder, spent more, flirted more. The two barmaids had their hands full, balancing trays of bottles and glasses as they circled the tables, skillfully avoiding the pinches aimed at their rumps.

Beth stood behind the counter and observed the bustling scene.

"Miss B.," a short black man called from the domino table, "drinks on the house tonight? Is holiday, you know."

Laughter rang out through the bar. Beth folded her arms over her ample bosom. "Maas Joe, don't make me come over there to you, you know. You still owe me from last month. Wait, your pay day don't come yet?"

Joe's domino partners chuckled and one of them slapped him on the back. "You must pay up you bills, man. You throw the biggest offering in church and can't pay you bill?"

"Cho, man, play you han' and stop bother me. You think I don't know you owe Miss B., too?"

Beth shook her head and smiled as she watched the men lose themselves again in the game. She had opened this bar nineteen years ago and had watched it grow from a one-room business to a two storey concrete building.

In the early days the church people had condemned her for opening such an establishment in Bonny Gate. She was not going to let church people decide what she would do, nor would she let them restrict her ability to take care of her child. She knew the bar would make money for her and she planned to take full advantage of the opportunity.

Yes, it had hurt when the church women passed her on the street and turned up their noses. Worse, it was a great embarrassment when she heard that she had been the subject of the sermon that week. But she was not going to let anyone determine the direction of her life. They could go ahead and preach and sermonize. That was their business. Despite all that, Beth knew what she had to do and she was determined to survive.

Two decades later she was one of the most successful businesswomen in the village and the same women who used to look down on her allowed their husbands to visit her bar. The Christmas when the head deaconess sent a note and asked her to donate a turkey for the church dinner Beth knew she had won.

"Yes, been one of the hottest years since sixty-two." Uriah Simmonds leaned back in his chair, rum glass in hand, ready to talk politics.

"Every year been hot since Independence, Maas Uriah." Jimmy, the butcher, took a sip of his beer and let out a loud belch.

"Bwoy, no year hot like this year. You know them say so far is over six hundred political murders take place already?" Uriah looked round the room and nodded emphatically. "These politicians haffi do better than that, you know. Is them bringing in all the guns and weapons into this place and making people killing off them one another."

"An' you know what the sad thing is?" Hubert Brown, Beth's neighbour, chimed in. "None a fi them pickney not dying in dis war. Is fi we pickney a dead off."

The discussion was animated and soon the entire room was involved. Beth just sat on her bar stool and watched as the usual defenders of the Jamaica Labour Party lambasted the People's National Party supporters for the state of the economy while the PNP group accused the Jamaica Labour Party of sabotaging the elections and 'mashing up the country' with propaganda and violence.

This was the norm. Politics was usually the discussion of the day and, if it was not politics, it was women. Beth had heard all this so many times that she was immune to the shouts, the boisterous laughter, the angry retorts, even the blows with which were thrown every once in a while. Her only stipulation was that fights be taken out into the streets - she had not worked this hard for drunkards to destroy her place.

It was almost two in the morning when the last of the patrons staggered out of the bar. It had been a good night. The holiday spirit had relaxed the men, loosened their grips on their pockets and whet their thirst for drink.

The barmaids left tired but satisfied with their night's earnings. A smile here, a touch there, and the tips became more generous. They knew how to work the bar. They knew how to get a semi-intoxicated man to slip his last dollar into their hands while he grabbed at their skirts.

As soon as the young women were gone Beth pushed the door shut and locked it. She climbed the narrow stairs to the second floor where she lived. As she lay down on the bed she sighed. She was not looking forward to the stress that would come when she got up at dawn.

Despite a throbbing headache Beth was up at six o'clock. It was a cool, sweet-smelling country morning and she was glad for the fresh air to clear her head. She had a lot to do and could not afford the luxury of lying in bed late.

She went out onto the balcony of her second floor bedroom and looked down the hill at the marl road and thick green foliage below. Birds warbled in the bushes and the early morning fog was beginning to lift so that she could almost make out Port Maria Bay in the distance.

"Miss Betty!"

Beth looked down to see Glenda Common walking slowly along the road below, leading her donkey loaded down with two hampers covered with crocus bags.

"How is the morning, Miss G.?" Beth smiled back and waved.

"All is well, Miss B., all is well." Glenda waved back. "What you want me bring back from bush for you? I goin' dig some yam head today and the pumpkin look like them ready."

"Thanks, Miss G., but I'm alright. I still have two pound o' the yam from last week."

Glenda waved her goodbye, switched the donkey on the rump, and went on her way.

It was just about time for Maas Hubert to pass this way too but, as usual, he would be trying to sneak past the house without greeting her. He, like many of the men in the village, had a tab at the bar. But that was not the problem. He had also borrowed two thousand dollars from her with the promise to pay her back by the end of that month. That was almost a year ago.

Beth was too tired to fight any battles this morning so, to save herself the effort and save him the embarrassment, she turned and went back into the bedroom and began to prepare for the day.

By eleven o'clock she had finished the Sunday dinner. She had prepared brown stewed fish with rice and peas and a macaroni pie. She also had a sweet potato pudding she had made two days before. She packed the food into neat little containers then stuffed them into her big shoulder bag. After making a final check of the stove she turned and pulled the door shut behind her then headed down the hill.

The one mile walk did her good. She walked with ease down the uneven road because it was one she knew like the back of her hand. Beth had been born in this community and was familiar with most of the people.

For a period in her life she had gone away. After departing at fourteen years old she had not beheld the place again until she was forty-one. Even so, it was still home to her. That was nineteen years ago and she never regretted returning.

One thing she did regret, though, was not returning for her father's funeral. He had passed away when she was twenty-eight years old. He had suffered from high blood pressure for many years but the stroke came suddenly. There was no second chance for him. He was dead at fifty-eight.

Although Beth had been away and had hardly kept in touch with the people of the village, or even her family, she had heard that he had fathered two children by his second wife. He had left her mother years before and started a new life with Loretta Moore, the postmistress. She remembered the years when she had desperately wanted to be a part of her father's life but had never heard from him. It was as if she no longer existed.

As Beth turned off the main road onto the dirt track that led to the neighbouring community she cleared her mind of the memory of the man she had loved so much. She shifted her bag to the other shoulder and climbed the hill to her mother's house.

The little green house looked almost the same way it had forty-six years ago when she had left Bonny Gate to go to work in Kingston. It was the same deep green with brown trimming and there was a big mahogany door in the centre. The paint was peeling in places and it was obvious that new paint had been slapped over old. The only additions that had been done were the kitchen and the bathroom which were now a part of the new building.

When Beth was a child they'd had to use the outhouse and all the cooking had taken place in a little shack fifteen yards away. She remembered the chilly morning visits to the outhouse and the bother of treading back and forth between the house and the kitchen with pots and pans and food.

But it was nineteen eighty now, and practically all the houses had electricity as well as indoor plumbing. No one had the time or the patience for the old life.

Beth climbed the steep steps, making sure to hold on to the rail, and rested her bag on the porch. She tapped gently at the door. There was no answer. She frowned then tapped again.

"Coming!" A cheerful, sing-song voice rang out then the door opened to reveal a plump, coffee-coloured young woman with rollers in her hair.

"Morning, Jennifer," Beth greeted her. "I was wondering if you were still in bed or something."

"No, Miss Beth. I was out back chopping coconuts."

"So why you chopping coconuts and you know I'm bringing the Sunday dinner?"

"I know, Miss Beth, but it was some coconut drops I was planning to make this evening. The school children, them love it, you see!"

Beth gave a grunt then pushed past the girl and went inside where she set her bag on the dining room table.

She turned to Jennifer. "What I tell you about leaving Mama here all by herself to go down to the school? You know I don't like it. What if, as you leave the house, she get up and stumble or something like that?"

"But I don't stay long, Mam. I only go down when I know they have recess and that's from about ten o'clock to about ten-thirty. Then I head right back."

"Jennifer," Beth's voice was firm as she glared at the woman who was no longer smiling, "if you don't get your act together I going to kick you out of here. You just watch yourself, you hear me? Get one of your little sisters to carry the drops down there but don't you leave my mother alone in this house."

"Yes, Miss Beth." Jennifer's face was sullen but she said nothing more. She turned and walked towards the kitchen.

Beth watched her retreating back then turned towards the main bedroom. As she entered the smell of Vicks VapoRub and Tiger Balm assailed her nostrils. The curtains were drawn and the room was in darkness.

"Mama? You up?"

"Elizabeth? That's you?" A frail voice responded from the corner. "You come already?" Irene Gordon sat in a rocking chair, covered in blankets.

"Mama, why you like to sit in the dark?" Beth went over to the window and pulled the curtains apart. The sudden flood of light made the old woman blink.

"Whether it dark or light it don't matter to me anymore," she sighed.

"Stop saying that," Beth said as she lifted the latch on the window and flung it wide open. "At least you can get some sun and some fresh air. Feel how in here hot. You want to die of heat stroke? It's almost midday and this place feels like an oven."

"Lord, why you letting in the draught?" was her mother's response. "Suppose you make me take up bad cold?"

"A little fresh air not going to kill you. You lock up yourself in the house too much, man."

Beth went and sat on the foot of the bed and looked at her mother. The strong curve of the woman's cheek had disappeared long ago and had been replaced by sagging folds of flesh. White hair peeked out from under her head wrap and she clutched at the blankets with flaccid arms.

But the greatest change had been in her eyes, which now stared vacantly in front of her. The deep brown eyes which used to draw such admiration were now hidden behind clouds. Those eyes would never see again.

"How you feeling today, Mama?"

"Well," Irene sighed, "the arthritis not too bad but the sugar high. I can feel my skin scratching me."

"Jennifer giving you your medication on time?"

"That girl, Jennifer, is a real trial. She wake up late so I can't get my breakfast on time and although she supposed to give me the medication she forget sometimes. I don't know why I have that little gal in my house." The old woman scowled and pursed her withered lips. "When her Mumma run her from the house I don't know why you take her in. She's a worthless, good-for-nothing little gal. You better just send her back home, you hear."

Beth listened to her mother's complaints but only shook her head. She knew that Jennifer was an airhead but she was not that bad. Her mother was getting senile and it was becoming more and more evident everyday. For her, everything was an exaggeration, but especially her resentment for the girl.

For Beth, these visits to her mother's house were painful events. Each Sunday she watched her mother decline further into the darkness of senility. On top of that, every day that she came to the house and saw Jennifer she remembered her own pain when her mother had sent her to work for Mrs. Henley in Kingston. She remembered the confusion, the hurt, the feeling of having been abandoned. She remembered the nights when she had wept alone in someone else's house, someone else's bed, miles away from the little green house in which she had been born.

In Jennifer she saw herself, and although she was tough with the young girl she never spoke down to her, never disrespected her. She wanted Jennifer to be tough just like she'd had to be. To survive as a woman in Jamaica you had to be tough.

"Mama, you hear from Gloria or Fred?"

"No, me dear," her mother sighed, "is only Simon sen' a little something in the post the other day. Jennifer read the letter to me and it had a fifty dollar US cheque. She get Glendon fi put it in the account for me yesterday."

Beth gritted her teeth. Of her mother's five children she was the only one who still lived in Jamaica. Gloria and Fred had both migrated to England in the nineteen fifties and Simon had left ten years ago to get married in America. Albert, her oldest brother and second in the family, had died in the sixties from lung cancer. They had all gone, every last one of them, leaving her with the responsibility of caring for their blind, diabetic, arthritic, close to senile mother. They, the ones her mother had loved, the ones she had kept close to her while she was shipped off to Kingston, were nowhere around when their mother needed them most.

And now it had fallen on her to be her mother's main source of support. Yes, they sent money, but not regularly. And where were they when she needed to go to the doctor, when she had one of her spells of depression, when she wanted to talk? Sometimes Beth wondered why she had bothered to move back to Bonny Gate. It would have been interesting to know what the others would have done with their mother if she had never come back to the village.

Beth continued to stare at her mother who seemed to have drifted off into a light doze. As she looked at her she wondered what she had done to this woman for her to have found it so easy to give her up.

Her mind went back to the day she had stormed out of Mrs. Henley's house. Her heart tightened at the memory. It was as if it were yesterday. Ignoring Mrs. Henley's face Beth had rushed down the walkway and through the gate without looking back. She ran until, exhausted, she flopped down on a bench at the nearby bus-stop. An old lady who was standing there looked at her quizzically but Beth ignored her.

She sat panting, both in exhaustion and terror. She did not know where she was going to go from here. The only thing she knew was that she was never going back to that house.

By the time the old woman had boarded a bus, leaving her alone at the bus stop, the reality had begun to sink in. How in God's name was she going to survive? She could not go back to the Henleys and she had vowed never to return to her mother's house. They had put her out and she was going to show them that she could do without them. At fifteen years old she would have to become a woman in an instant.

As people came and went, Beth sat pondering her situation. Before she knew it over two hours had passed and she still had not devised a plan. She knew very few people in Kingston and none of those could help her.

Then her mind went back to old Mrs. Plunkett who lived down the street from the Henleys. She was a retired teacher who had loaned her a few books. Mrs. Plunkett must have seen Beth's desire to learn, her determination to survive. She was always encouraging her to come over to her house and browse through her many shelves of books. This kind woman was her only hope. With a heavy sigh she stood up and headed back in the direction from which she had come.

Thirty minutes later Beth was sitting in the old lady's living room, relating everything that had happened.

"What are you saying to me, child?" Mrs. Plunkett's usually serene face was frozen in shock. "Are you telling me the truth?"

As the tears rolled down her cheeks, Beth sobbed, "Is true, Miss Plunkett. I would never lie to you, Mam."

"Get my walking stick, girl. We are going down to that house right now. "

"But I don't want to go back there!"

"We can't let that man get away with this. I have to put a stop to it. I wonder how many young girls he has put this kind of thing to?" Mrs. Plunkett's heavy bosom heaved with her anger. She grabbed the walking stick from Beth's hand, shrugged into her sweater and walked off, leaving Beth to follow behind her.

It was an ugly scene. Mr. Henley never came out of the house but his wife came out to the front porch. As soon as she saw Mrs. Henley, Mrs. Plunkett blasted her. Mrs. Henley defended her husband but she was unconvincing. It was as if she was just saying the words out of duty to him.

Beth stood on the steps behind Mrs. Plunkett but she could see Mrs. Henley's eyes, the way they shifted away from Mrs. Plunkett's glare, the way they turned down to her feet as if she were ashamed. Beth almost felt sorry for her. Almost.

Mrs. Plunkett threatened to report the incident to the police but Beth spoke up at that point.

"Is alright, Mam. I jus' want my things."

While they waited on the porch Mrs. Henley called to Mildred to bring the bag with Beth's few belongings. Within minutes Beth and Mrs. Plunkett were leaving the Henley house.

The next five years went by in a blur for Beth. She stayed with Mrs. Plunkett for almost two years, assisting the elderly woman in the small nursery school she ran. But then she died and Beth had to find another way to survive.

At age seventeen she again found herself on the streets of Kingston with nowhere to go. She had not been back to Bonny Gate all this time and had only received one letter from her mother, through Miss Mildred. She never replied.

When Mrs. Plunkett's relatives came to claim the house Beth moved on. With the little money she had saved while working there she rented a room on Maxfield Avenue and began to look for work. During her first year she survived by doing 'day's work': cleaning, cooking and washing.

Luckily, Mrs. Plunkett had been a very religious woman and many of her church sisters had visited the house continually. It was from this group of church women that Beth was able to get her first clients. She worked so well that eventually she was recommended to other people and she soon had consistent work. But still, the money was never enough. She was barely able to survive.

Then her big break came. A bar opened up on the street on which she lived and she was one of the first women to turn up on the doorstep, looking for work. By this time she was eighteen years old and had been independent for three years. She was young but her maturity and experience of life must have shone through her youth. She got the job.

With two incomes life began to improve for Beth. She was able to rent a slightly bigger place but continued to live on the same street. She did not want to move too far away from her new place of employment, especially because she had to find her way home alone at night.

It was a lonely existence because she was not the outgoing type and had few friends. Looking back, she wondered if that was why she fell so easily for the first man who showed any interest in her, the first one who ever expressed admiration for her.

Their meeting was different from the usual bar conversations where men would compliment her figure and looks and even try to get physical. She knew how to handle that. This man was different. He actually made her blush. And when he looked at her, Beth's heart did a funny thing - it actually hurt.

It all started when Devon offered to walk her home one night. He was a real gentleman, never once trying to touch her, not even when they arrived at the house. She had actually thought about inviting him in but then thought better of it, and he never asked. She was glad.

But the next time he walked her home he did ask her for a kiss and she let him have it. It was hard to say no to the tall honey-coloured man with the narrow moustache and the hint of a beard on his chin, who stared down at her with light brown eyes fringed with thick eyelashes.

But it was not how he looked that got to Beth, it was what he said and how he said it. He was the only man who ever spoke to her in proper English and he actually called her by her full name, Elizabeth. It made her feel special.

As they held hands at nights while he walked her home, he would say, "Elizabeth, my sweet". Then she would giggle and reply, "Devon, my prince."

It was five weeks before Devon saw the inside of her room and another eight before she could drum up the courage to 'be a woman', as he called it.

Three months later she realized she was pregnant.

"I don't believe this," were the first words out of Devon's mouth when Beth told him. "I thought you knew how to prevent this."

"Prevent this? But I don't know nothing 'bout these things."

"So, you don't talk to other women? They always know how to mix up different things to take so they don't get pregnant. Which bush did you come from, where they don't teach you these things?"

Beth remained silent, shocked at the disdain in his voice. He had never before used that tone to her.

"Devon, you tell me you know everything about this. You say you would teach me." Beth fought back the tears as she looked up at him. "You never say anything to me 'bout taking something to prevent babies."

"But I thought you knew. This is something that women know about. I should not have to tell you this."

Beth looked down and a tear slid down her cheek. "Well…nobody never tell me."

Beth sat on the chair and peered up at Devon. He looked almost as confused as she felt. She hated to see him like this, the man who had always seemed so strong, so capable, so sure. But worse, she hated feeling the way she did - confused and desperate.

Even when she had gone through her darkest moments she had always felt that she had control of her life - but not now. What was she going to do with a baby?

Devon stood rubbing his forehead then he looked down at Beth. "I have a question to ask you. And don't get angry." His tone was serious and somehow Beth knew that what would come next would not be nice.

"Elizabeth. Are you sure this baby is mine?"

At first, Beth did not understand the question. "Sure? Yeah. I can't make no baby by myself."

Devon shoved his fists into his pockets and paced the room then he stopped in front of her again and, staring intently at her, repeated the question.

"Are you sure this baby is mine? Are you telling me that I am the only man you have ever had? There is no one else?"

Finally, his meaning began to sink in. Beth's mouth fell open in surprise then she snapped her jaws shut in anger. She stood to her full five feet, seven inches and glared at the man across the room.

"What you think I am? Some kind of whore? You think, because I live downtown, all I do is sleep around with man? You well know that you was the first man I ever have, the one and only man, and you have the gall to come put question to me 'bout, if you is the father of my child?"

For a moment Devon looked ashamed then he said, "I want to believe you, Beth, but when I am gone during the days I don't know what happens behind my back. You're a nice girl and everything, but it's not like we see each other every day, and anything can happen when my back is turned. You're a sexy girl and I know that you have a lot of men running you down. Look at how they behave around you down by the bar? I just don't want to find myself caught in some trap because I slept with you a few times."

Beth sucked in her breath sharply. His words were like a slap in the face. This was all it had been to him, brief moments of pleasure, release for his desire, nothing more. She could have kicked herself for believing that there could have been anything else between them. She was nothing more than his little downtown, ghetto girl.

The confirmation came when he blurted out, "In fact, the few times we did it, I don't even think anything happened. I think you're trying to pull a fast one on me. You know I'm in my final year at college. You think I want to be trapped with a child right now? If that is your way of holding on to me, you can forget it."

Beth listened to his callous speech and remained silent for a long while. Finally, she spoke. "Devon, leave my house. Never come back here. In fact, don't even bother coming by the bar anymore. You told me one time that you and I are from different worlds. Well, now I understand what you mean. You go back to your world, free and clear, and don't worry 'bout nothing. I will stay in mine." With that, she rose from the chair, went to the door and opened it wide. She stared coldly at him as he looked sheepish and shuffled his way out the door. She closed it behind him with a click.

By the time Leonie was old enough to start asking about a father Beth had devised the best story she could. She told the five-year-old that her father had been killed on a fishing trip before she was even born.

That story kept her daughter quiet until her teens when more questions came. Where was her grandmother? Where were her father's relatives? Why had she never met any of them? It was at that point that Beth decided to tell Leonie the truth. And it was only then that she let herself feel the pain of rejection from the only man she had ever loved.

Leonie was her saving grace, keeping her sane all those years she was struggling to survive. The child was her reason for living. Her family had rejected her then Devon had done the same. Why should she expect anything more from the world? But she was determined to give her child everything that she never had. And no matter what, she would never abandon her.

Mr. Williams, the owner of the bar, had been kind enough to let her work until her stomach started to show and then he had let her come back after her baby was born. She had survived during those months without work because she had saved every penny that she could. Mr. Williams also got the workers at the bar to put together and buy her baby supplies. They even gave her an envelope with some money.

When Beth returned to work she left the baby with a neighbour but it soon became too much and, to her regret, she had to give up her job at the bar. But Mr. Williams had connections and he was able to secure her a position in a factory nearby. During the days when she went to work she left the baby at the church daycare centre and, understanding her situation, they never pressured her for money. She paid when she could.

Beth was relieved when Leonie was old enough to go to school. At least she knew she would be safe and occupied until three in the afternoon. This was fine for her as she had requested to be on the morning shift and she got off work at two. Beth's life was finally falling into place.

It was also because of Leonie that Beth decided to go to night school. She knew if she were going to be able to provide for her child and give her the type of education she wanted, she would have to get better jobs. Working in a factory was never going to pay her enough to send Leonie to private school.

Her daughter turned six in August of nineteen forty-four and by September Beth had signed up for classes. It took her five years of study, on and off, but at the end of it she had a diploma in secretarial studies and a certificate in business management.

By the end of the programme she was full of ideas on setting up her own business but she knew it would take time and money and so she used her new qualifications to go job hunting.

When Leonie was in the third grade Beth secured a position as a representative in Barclays Bank. Nine years later Leonie finished high school and was getting ready to enter teachers' college. By then Beth was a senior supervisor in her department.

When Leonie was finally in the classroom teaching Beth decided she'd had enough. She had worked hard all her life, first to survive on her own and then to ensure the education and survival of her child. She was sick of working for other people. It was time to move on.

At the age of forty-one Beth packed up and moved back to the country to start her life all over again. She had made it. On her own. Without a fancy education and without the help of family. No one could ever say they had done it for her. She had done it all on her own.

Quick tears burned her eyes and she blinked. She stared at her mother's sleeping form then her face crumbled. Silent tears ran down her cheeks. She was a grandmother now but she still could not get over the hurt. She could not understand why this woman, her own mother, had rejected her, turned her out. She had never explained why. All she had said was that she could not manage all those children. But why her?

With a sniff, Beth pulled herself together and dabbed at her tears. If her mother had been awake she would not have broken down in that manner. This was forty-six years later. What did it matter now? She was a sixty year old woman, for goodness sake. What could an eighty-seven year old woman approaching senility tell her at this stage in life?

Beth got up and leaned out the window, feeling the country breeze drying her cheeks. The green hills and trees were soothing. With a soft, sad smile, she turned from the window and went back to her mother and shook her gently.

"Ma," she whispered, "Wake up. It's time to eat."

Chapter 7

1987

Princess watched as the elderly woman poured the balance of the thick, white coconut milk into the Dutch pot. This was the last Sunday dinner she was going to have in Jamaica before she headed out for New York. Her grandmother was making her favourite dish - steamed fish and okra with rice and peas. She was also going to get fried plantain on the side. Her mouth watered just thinking about it. She could hardly wait.

Lionel and her mother would join them in a little while and they would all sit down to her farewell dinner.

"Grandma, you must take good care of yourself while I'm gone. I don't like to have to worry about you, you know. Why don't you move in with Mommy, like she said?"

"Aah, me chile. I'm glad you think about your grandmother, but I will be alright. I may be getting up in age but I not fool-fool yet."

"Grandma, is not a matter of fool-fool. I'm just thinking about your safety."

"I understand, Baby, but I been on my own since I was fourteen years old. I have my independence for so long I can't give it up now. I like it this way. I'm not going to live under somebody else's roof unless I absolutely have to, not even if is my own daughter. And may the good Lord take me by the time I have to go depend on somebody else."

"Lord, Grandma, don't talk like that."

The conversation was interrupted by a knock on the door. Princess got up and went to open it. It was the little girl from next door. She was sucking on a lollipop.

Princess held the door open and she entered. She popped the lollipop out of her mouth and walked over to where Beth was stirring the heavy pot. "Mother Beth, Mama say to ask you if you have any cake soap, you can len' her one."

Princess rolled her eyes and mumbled under her breath, "Think is shop we have over here."

Beth frowned briefly at her granddaughter but smiled at the little girl and said, "Yes, dear, just wait a minute."

She went to the back of the house, leaving Princess with the little girl.

"So, what is your name?" Princess asked just to kill time until her grandmother returned.

"Jennifer, Mam."

"Why you calling me Mam? I look like old woman to you?"

"No, Mam."

Princess sighed in disgust and turned away. She was glad to see Grandma Beth returning, cake soap in hand.

"Remind your mother to send back my waiter that she borrow for the wedding, you hear?"

"Yes, Mam."

After the little girl had left Princess sat down again at the kitchen table and pulled on her ponytail. "It's a tray, Grandma, not a waiter," she said, grinning. "And why these people always have to send to you for things?"

"Is so you must live, chile. No man is an island. And, by the way, just check your dictionary and you will see that I can use the word 'waiter'. Sometimes you just too smart." Beth smiled and pinched her granddaughter's plump cheek.

They heard the sound of a motor vehicle approaching. "Mom's here!" Princess yelled and went out to the verandah. The car was parked at the bottom of the hill so she ran down the pathway to meet her mother. The path was lined with Joseph Coats, Crotons and Zinnias. Her grandmother loved flowers and had planted them all over the yard.

Her prize possessions were her roses which she had planted right under the window sill. They were blooming red, pink and yellow and they were beautiful. As Princess ran the dogs followed her, barking and yelping and playing. They scared the goat which was tied to the breadfruit tree by the front gate.

"Move. Go back to the house!" Princess threw pebbles at the dogs but they dodged the tiny missiles and kept on running and barking. She gave up chasing them away and stopped, instead, to comfort the skittish goat.

Lionel and their mother came up the pathway towards her. Her mother was wearing a pair of dark blue jeans and a white shirt. Her hair had been cut short and she was wearing curls. Now in her fifties, Leonie had put on weight, and was now over a hundred and forty pounds. Her face still looked fresh and pleasant and it was easy to see that she was happy.

Lionel was tall and lanky, as usual, and the girls called him handsome. His moustache suited his slim face and his curly black hair gave him a very young appearance although he was already in his late twenties. The only resemblance he had to their mother was his long, straight face.

They all three walked together back to the house.

As they entered, Grandma Beth said, "Welcome to my humble abode."

"You say that every time, Grandma," Lionel said, smiling, then they all sat around the kitchen table, their favourite meeting place.

"So, Lionel, how is the work at Shell? You managing alright?"

"Yeah, Grandma. The work is good but the hours long, though. The good thing is that the pay not too bad. But still, if I come back in a next life, I probably would not choose to come back as an engineer. Maybe as a DJ." They all laughed.

He put his arm around Princess. "Little Sis, how you feel about going so far away to study? Excited?"

"Yeah, but…kinda scared, too."

"Don't be. You did well to get that scholarship and we're all proud of you." Leonie beamed as she gave Princess a pat on the shoulder. "We know you will excel."

"Well," Beth cut in, "I imagine we all ready to eat now. Princess, come help me share the food, Baby."

As they sat at the table and Grandma prayed for her safe travel, Princess's heart swelled with pride and love for her family.

Princess gripped the arms of the seat and closed her eyes as the plane took off. It was her first flight, she was alone and she was scared. She hoped no one was watching her. This was so embarrassing. When the plane finally levelled off she opened her eyes and heaved a sigh of relief. She was still in the sky but at least she was not hearing the engines roaring in her ears.

"Are you alright?" The Air Jamaica flight attendant smiled warmly at her and Princess smiled back.

"I'm okay, thanks."

"Would you like a glass of water?"

"Yes, please."

"First flight, huh?"

When Princess nodded she whispered, "Don't worry, you'll be fine."

Her uncle picked her up at John F. Kennedy Airport and soon they were on their way to his home in the Bronx. 'America,' Princess thought, 'I'm finally here!'

She had heard of the United States all her life – who in this world had not? – and she had always hoped to one day visit the land of American apples, Disney World and Michael Jackson. Many of her friends from high school had been to the 'States' several times to visit relatives or to go shopping.

She, however, had never really believed that she would ever make it here, not until she was a grown woman. Her mother would never have been able to afford to send her on such trips – not on a teacher's salary with two mouths to feed. She never complained, though. She knew her mother did her best for them and she was grateful. There were so many children in school who were in a worse position than they. Finally, her patience had paid off – now she was on terra firma in the land of the 'green bucks'.

"So, how have you been doing, Princess?"

Uncle Robert's voice broke into her thoughts. He was her father's brother, not a relative she knew very well, but her only family contact in New York. He glanced over at her as he drove. "Last time I saw you, you were just a little girl – just about six or seven years old. Now you're all grown up. Time certainly flies…"

"Yes, Uncle," she replied, "I'm eighteen now."

"And how is your mother?"

"She's fine, thanks, Uncle."

After that there was silence. They really did not have much to say to each other. Princess hardly knew him, having met him maybe only two times before. In fact, she had hardly had any contact with anybody on her father's side of the family. For her, he had been more like a distant uncle than a father. Her contact with him had been sporadic and her relationship with his relatives had been almost non-existent. But Princess did not mind the silence at all. With less conversation she could really focus on seeing the famous New York City at night.

New York City was not exactly what Princess had expected. Of course, she was impressed by the huge buildings and wide streets and so many different cars. What she had not expected to see was men and women in heavy coats with scarves covering everything except their eyes, standing around bonfires burning in metal drums, trying to keep warm. Neither had she expected to see huge cardboard boxes on the sidewalk, and on enquiring what purpose they served, to be told that people lived in them.

'In the winter?' she thought. 'They're going to freeze to death!'

At least in Jamaica it was warm all year round so the homeless did not have to deal with the bitter cold. And that was the other thing – why were there so many people on the streets? This was America, the land of plenty! People back home were all dying to come here. Those who had worked here were able to return home and buy big houses and live in good neighbourhoods. All she had ever heard about was all the Yankee dollars that could be made. No one had ever told her about this side of America. 'The grass may look greener on the other side,' she thought, 'but if you come close enough you can still see some patches of brown.'

Robert Ramjeet lived on the fifteenth floor of a beautiful apartment building. There was even a doorman to let them in. She had a moment's concern when they approached the elevator. She had been in one only once before when she had attended a ball at the Pegasus Hotel in Kingston. Elevators made her nervous. She gasped as it jerked then ascended. Her uncle looked at her quizzically but she averted her eyes. Her stomach almost felt like it had when she was on the plane. She was glad when the door opened and they got off.

That night she lay in bed for a long time, staring at the ceiling, thinking. She had had so many new experiences – her first airplane ride, her first view of America, her first night in bed in the great U.S. of A. The excitement kept her awake for a long time but when she finally drifted into slumber her thoughts were on the soft warmth of her grandmother's farewell hug.

Princess was nervous. The bus ride from the Bronx to her new school in upstate New York had been long and she had had lots of time to think about what lay ahead. What if she could not manage the school work? What if she ran out of money? What if she did not like her room-mate, or worse, what if her room-mate did not like her?

This last concern was foremost in her mind as she tapped nervously at the door to the room she would share with Stephanie Lowinski. Lowinski sounded like a white person's name. She had seen lots of white people when she was back home. She had had a white teacher from the Peace Corps when she was in the eighth grade and the principal's wife had been white. And of course, there were always lots of tourists visiting the island.

But she did not really know any white person well; she certainly had never had one for a friend. Now she would have to live with one. Not that she had a problem with that – it was just that she had seen so many movies about prejudice and discrimination in America that she was just a little bit scared. Well, she would just have to be tough and deal with it, she thought. With a sigh, she rapped on the door again.

"Coming."

The voice was muffled by the heavy door. There was the sound of a latch opening then a small, blonde-haired girl with sleepy blue eyes was peeking around the door.

"Yes?" She rubbed one eye and looked up at Princess through the other. She made Princess, at five feet six inches, feel like a giant. This girl did not even look like she was five feet tall. Neither did she look old enough to be in college.

"I'm Princess Ramjeet, your new room-mate." She tried to smile at the girl but she was too nervous.

The girl rubbed her eyes again then her face softened in a smile. "Oh, yes, the Resident Assistant told me to expect you."

She stepped back, pulling the door open, and beckoned to Princess to enter. "Sorry I seemed kinda grumpy but I was still half-asleep. We were out partying last night and I was beat." Her smile was both apologetic and mischievous at the same time. "Do you like to party?"

"Uh, yes," Princess said quickly, caught off-guard. Then she said hurriedly, "I mean no, not really." She watched the girl for a negative reaction but all she got was another grin.

"Make up your mind. Do you like to party or don't you?" Stephanie sat down on her bed by the window, tucked her feet underneath her, and stared openly at Princess as she struggled to unlock her suitcase.

Princess fiddled with the lock a while longer then said, "I don't know. I haven't been out much…but I love to dance."

Stephanie laughed. "Poor thing. You must be like I was a semester ago." Her mouth opened wide in a yawn and she stretched thin arms over her head. "When I got here in September I was so un-cool - never smoked a cig, never had a drink in my life! But I got into the hang of things real soon. Don't worry, Princess, I'll have you partying in no time."

"Uh, thanks," Princess replied, feeling doubtful.

"Here, let me help you with that." Stephanie jumped off the bed and went to kneel beside Princess. She grabbed the lock from her hand and jiggled the key until the lock popped open.

"There," she cried, triumphant. "Got it!"

"Th…thanks," said Princess, still surprised and relieved at how friendly her room-mate had turned out to be. Maybe things would not be so bad, after all.

Princess sat at a table in the corner watching the other students on the dance floor. Stephanie was dancing with her boyfriend. She had finally convinced Princess to come to the party although she had been very hesitant. She was still very shy and felt out of her league. She had been in America for three months now but still found it difficult to make new friends. Everyone here was so different from what she was used to. She was from a small town in Jamaica and although this college was small by American standards, she still felt she did not match up to these cosmopolitan people.

Also, she had already gained twelve pounds since she had been here. She had discovered pancakes and eggs and loved them so much that she ate them every morning for breakfast. She had already been a little plump when she left Jamaica three months ago but now her five feet six inch frame had to carry almost one hundred and sixty pounds.

She had always been self-conscious about her weight but now it was even worse. She felt huge whenever she and her petite room-mate went out together. What made it worse Stephanie always looked so pretty with her fancy clothes and perfect make-up. No matter how Princess tried, she could never fix her hair and face as nicely as her friend.

Tonight she was wearing a simple black dress and black pumps. Her only accessories were a gold chain and gold hoop earrings. She had also applied a little make-up. She sat in the semi darkness sipping a glass of iced tea, watching the students bobbing up and down on the dance floor.

"Want to dance?"

Princess looked up to see a young white man standing over her, grinning. Her heart fell. She had been hoping to disappear into the shadows, unnoticed.

"Me? I can't dance."

"Sure, you can. I heard you were from Jamaica. I don't know any Jamaican who doesn't know how to dance."

Princess only looked down at her hands, wishing the boy would just go away.

"Come on," he prodded, "you only live once."

When he just stood there, looking like he was never going to move, she rose and said softly, "Okay, I'll give it a try."

To Princess's surprise she found that she enjoyed being on the dance floor. Music pounded in her ears, disco lights flashed, and for the while she actually felt that she could dance. David seemed oblivious to her as he twisted his body and flailed his arms. He did not try to hold her. He was not even looking at her. But at least he was there in front of her, twisting and bobbing and making her feel like she was a part of this crazy, happy party scene.

It was not until about thirty minutes later when the music slowed and the lights dimmed that her partner took her arm and led her back to his table. Two blonde girls were already sitting there and they greeted him with friendly waves and smiles.

David pulled out a chair for Princess then said, "Hey, guys, this is Princess, all the way from Jamaica, mon!"

The girls giggled at his funny attempt at a Jamaican accent.

"Princess, meet Brittany and Ashley."

The girls smiled in greeting and Princess began to relax with the strangers. It was difficult to speak with the music playing but she did not mind. She just sat there, sipping her drink and rocking her body gently to the soft music. David kept smiling at her and so did the girls. Princess revelled in her new-found friendships.

It was not until the following week that Princess realized what a fool she had been. It had all been a big joke - on her! The rumours must have started circulating almost immediately but, loner that she was, Princess did not get wind of it until that Tuesday evening when she was working in the college library.

She sat typing labels for the stack of books in front of her when a tall black girl strode up to her. "I hope you learned your lesson."

Princess looked up at her, confused. "What lesson?"

The girl glared at her for a moment then her anger seemed to lift and she shook her head slowly. "You really don't know, do you?"

"Know what?" Princess was getting even more confused.

"It's all over the school…that David won the bet when he spent the whole evening dancing with 'Miss Piggy'.

Princess felt like she had just been slapped in the face.

The girl continued. "Two cheerleaders dared David to dance with the ugliest girl in the room and they decided that with your big body and pug nose, you were it."

Princess felt faint. She felt the blood rise to her face and her heart slowed in anguish.

As the girl watched her reaction she must have realized how devastating this revelation was to Princess. Her face softened and she said gently, "You should have guessed something was fishy when one of the most popular boys in the school asked you to dance. It's not as if he doesn't have all kinds of girls running after him."

Princess had heard enough. Without another word she got up from the computer and walked away.

Back in her room a tear ran down her cheek as she sat looking at herself in the mirror. Her usually golden skin had become paler with the winter weather. Her thick, wavy hair was loose and fell to the middle of her back. Curls framed her heart-shaped face. Her dark brown eyes were fringed with thick black lashes, and her lips were a naturally rosy pink. Altogether, not a bad looking face, she thought, except for that curse of a pug nose.

Princess bemoaned the fact that, of all the things she could have inherited from her mother, it was her nose that she got. She was often called 'the spitting image' of her father - except for the nose that vividly displayed her African blood.

And then there was the problem of her weight. Neither her mother nor her father was fat but she had learned that her long-dead paternal grandmother had been a short, fat Indian woman. Of course, she would have had to take after that grandparent, wouldn't she?

With a hiccup she wiped her eyes and resolved never to leave her room again except when absolutely necessary.

Princess knew that everyone around her noticed the difference in her demeanour, but especially Stephanie. She became cold and withdrawn but she made no apologies. If they wanted a reason to dislike her, she thought, she would give it to them.

The more withdrawn Princess became the better she did in her school work. Every moment alone was spent studying so that she was soon making straight A's in all her classes. Her greatest satisfaction came when her teachers praised her publicly for scoring the highest in her tests. She was the top student in every class she took.

I may not be beautiful, she thought, but I'm going to show them I'm one of the smartest students on campus. None of them, she decided, not the stupid cheerleaders, not David, not his stupid friends, would get a higher GPA than she would.

Princess's hard work paid off. By the end of the semester she had earned the respect of her classmates on the small campus. Her proudest moment was when she was awarded the Ethan Gregory Smith Award for Excellence in Academics. She was the first foreigner at the school to ever receive this award and she was ecstatic.

But, to Princess's dismay, the recognition brought challenges she never dreamed of. She was surprised when the lecturer in Communications called her into his office one day.

"How would you like to head the school's debating team," he asked.

"Me?" she squeaked. "Why me?"

"Why not you?" He smiled at her. "You're our best student in speech and communications and we want only the best to lead the team. Will you do it?"

"I don't know, Dr. Sloan. What if they don't listen to me? What if they don't like me?" Her voice rose. "I can't do it. They hate me."

"Calm down, Princess. Nobody hates you."

"They do."

"What's wrong? Is there something you would like to tell me?" The concern was evident on Dr. Sloan's face. "Why are you getting so emotional about this?"

"They…they think I'm ugly," Princess said in a low voice as she stared at the floor, "and they all hate me for it."

"Have a seat, Princess." Dr. Sloan rose and pulled out a chair. "We need to talk."

At Donald Sloan's prodding Princess described the terrible humiliation she had experienced at the hands of her college mates.

The man's face turned grim. Then he spoke. "Listen to me. You are one of the most well known, well respected students on this campus. You are destined to go far, to be a leader. None of the people you mentioned has achieved half of what you've done. Don't you ever let anyone take away your fire and don't let any halfwit tell you you're not beautiful."

He folded his arms across his chest and looked at her with serious eyes. "Princess, you have to stop comparing yourself to others. If you spend your life comparing you will always find people who are more beautiful than you, and you will find people who are less beautiful. You'll also find people who are more intelligent than you and others who are less intelligent. You have to put the comparisons aside and just make sure that you are the best Princess Ramjeet that you can be. The world will thank you for it, and you will thank yourself."

Princess sat there, her eyes still downcast. What her teacher was saying made sense to her but it still did not lessen the pain of being ridiculed.

When she remained silent Dr. Sloan continued. "Before you can fulfill your true potential you have to learn to love yourself, Princess. Don't let anyone short-circuit you now."

Princess lifted her eyes to the man's rugged face and nodded slowly. He looked so concerned that she gave him a weak smile. "Thanks, Dr. Sloan. I'll…I'll try to be strong."

As she rose to leave he walked over to the door and held it open for her. "Remember what I said. You can't truly love anyone else unless you first love yourself. Go find your beauty."

The next semester flew by for Princess. She was determined not to disappoint her mentor. Swallowing her fear she selected her team and began to prepare. Her days were full and long. Heading the debating team was one of the best things that could have happened to her. St. Richards College became number one in New York State and she was known in several college circles.

She had become so busy that her daily diet of pancakes and eggs became a thing of the past. All she had time to do was grab an apple on her way to classes in the mornings. Without realizing it she lost almost twenty pounds. She no longer stared miserably at herself in the mirror. She did not have the time. She was too busy debating, working on campus, keeping her grades high and participating in all the new activities she had signed up for.

In addition to all that Princess was registered with the college as a tutor of English, Spanish and Calculus. She had to be present in the tutoring room every Tuesday and Thursday evening from five to seven, making herself available to any student who came in for help with these subjects.

One evening she sat reading in the tutoring room, waiting to see if anyone would show up. Just half an hour before the session was scheduled to end a thin girl entered the room, wearing dark glasses.

Princess greeted her warmly. "Hi. What can I help you with?"

She pointed to the chair and indicated to the visitor that she should have a seat. Although she had received no verbal response Princess continued to smile then said, "First time I've seen you here. I'm Princess, and you are?"

"Ashley…Ashley Stewart."

"So, Ashley, which subject would you like to work on?"

The girl remained oddly silent and Princess began to wonder if something was wrong with her. Then she took off her dark glasses. Princess sucked in her breath as she looked into the sunken eyes of the girl who had so cruelly humiliated her over a year ago.

One look was all Princess needed to realize that the girl was anorexic. Her face was so thin her cheekbones protruded and the shadows around her eyes made her look like a ghost. Princess saw thin wrists protruding from the cuffs of her shirt. The girl's sweater hung from her almost fleshless frame.

"Ashley…what happened?" Princess was so shocked at the girl's transformation that she didn't know what else to say.

"Don't you worry about me," Ashley snarled, "I'm only here because my college advisor said it's mandatory. I need to get my English grades up."

Princess pursed her lips, taken aback by the girl's aggressiveness. She could have an attitude, too. After all, she was the one who had been hurt by the dirty prank played by Ashley and her shallow friends. But then, she thought, what was the use? It was water under the bridge now.

"Well, okay," she said casually, "let's get started."

That evening was the start of a month of sessions with Ashley and the formation of a relationship of sorts between the two. To Princess's surprise she ended up offering not only tutoring services to the young woman but also advice.

It turned out that, beneath the surface, Ashley was just as insecure as she used to be. After a few sessions Ashley began to open up to Princess and finally revealed her pain at never being able to live up to her parents' high standards. Her father was a successful attorney and her mother, a theatre actress, and she worried that she would never be as successful, or famous, or as beautiful as they expected her to be. She hated being an only child. There was just too much pressure on her to be perfect. She was never good enough. Now, she was beginning to actually hate going home to see her parents.

Ashley's distress was so great that Princess felt sorry for her. She wished she could do something to help her. One evening, as they were going over one of Ashley's essays, Princess decided to share with her the most important lesson she had learned in life so far.

She took the paper from the other girl's hand and began to speak. "Ashley, I know how you can finally be happy."

Ashley looked back at her expectantly but said nothing.

When she remained silent Princess pressed on. "You have to stop trying to prove your worth to your parents. Stop comparing yourself to them and love yourself instead." She took Ashley's hand. "You have to learn to love yourself before you can truly love anyone else…"

Chapter 8

2002

"Christian!"

Before he could react Christian felt a sharp slap on his back. As he turned he saw his friend Robert's grinning face.

"What up?" Christian grinned back at him.

"Nothing much. Where you going now?"

"The library. Remember that homework that Mrs. Brown gave us for next term? I want to start looking at it now."

"Bwoy, you goody-goody, eh? Why you starting on that so early?"

"Maybe it's because I don't know what the heck I'm going to write about. Jamaican heritage? I don't know nothing 'bout that. I goin' to see if I can get some ideas at the library. What you going to do your project on?"

"Karate!"

"Be serious. What karate have to do with Jamaican heritage?"

"Well, I can talk about how I karate a man at the Independence Festival."

"Stop you noise," Christian laughed. "You too fool-fool sometimes."

Robert fell into step with Christian and they both trod along the dusty road towards the local library. They had been friends since the second grade. They were nothing alike. Where Christian was dark and slim, Robert was light-skinned and stocky. Christian wore glasses and tended to be more reserved. Robert, on the other hand, was always jovial, loud, and funny. They were the perfect complement for each other.

"Christian, you saw the latest Jackie Chan movie?"

"No. You know my mother won't let me go to the movies."

"Bwoy you salt, eeh man? You don't know what you missing."

"Yeah, yeah. So what's so great about this movie?"

"It just bad! Nuff action and kicking and stuff like that. And nuff jokes, too." Robert paused then looked at Christian. "How come your last name is Lee and you don't even like karate? You're a disgrace to your name. You could be Bruce Lee's cousin, for all you know."

Christian laughed. "I doubt it."

Robert gave Christian a shove then dashed off ahead of him. Christian ran after him, howling a Red Indian war cry as he went.

It was almost six o'clock before they left the library that evening. They would have to walk a quarter of a mile to get to the bus stop but they did not mind. Sitting at the desk in the library, poring over books for hours, had taken its toll. They were tired of it and needed some physical activity.

As they walked Robert kept up a running commentary about the Jackie Chan movie. He demonstrated his Kung Fu moves and even tried one or two blows on Christian who sidestepped them then ran at him, trying a few moves of his own. They jostled each other as they walked, pretending not to see the glares of the adults who watched their childish play as they walked along the road.

Christian drew in a sharp breath. He grabbed Robert's arm. Heading in their direction were three rough-looking boys wearing red, green and gold arm bands.

"What?" Still grinning, Robert turned to Christian and gave him a playful shove.

"It's them," Christian whispered, "the Black Star Crew."

Robert's smile disappeared. He turned in the direction of Christian's stare. The older boys were walking purposefully towards them. Christian could feel his heart tighten and his palms get damp. Robert shifted closer to him.

"Hey, black Chiney! Whe' you a do pon de road dis time a day?"

The smaller boys were silent. They just stood there looking down at the ground, avoiding any eye contact with their tormentors.

"Hey, bwoy! You nuh hear big man a talk to you?" The big boys were right in front of them now.

"And what 'bout you, Piggy? Why you nuh stop eat?"

Robert's light skin turned red but he remained silent. Christian could feel the sweat trickling from his armpits. It pricked the back of his neck.

He had been down this road many times before. Ever since he had entered high school this group of boys had targeted him. He was usually the brunt of their jokes. Robert was just a casualty because he was in Christian's company.

Still staring at his feet, Christian mumbled, "Why don't you leave us alone?"

"What?" The largest of the boys took a step forward. "You say something, worm?"

Christian drew in a trembling breath. "I said, leave us alone."

The bigger boy stared at Christian for a brief moment then burst out laughing. "The mawga bwoy think him can give orders 'round this place. You hear him, me brethren?"

They all laughed at the joke.

Without warning, the beefy boy grabbed Christian by the collar and dragged him up to his hairy face.

"You think me romping with you, bwoy? You chat to big man with respect, you hear me?"

He shoved Christian away from him, almost causing him to fall backwards. He shoved his fist in his pocket and rocked back and forth.

"Next time oonu see we," he snarled, "oonu scatta!"

Without a backward glance he sauntered off with his cronies in tow.

"Sheesh," Robert whispered as he watched the boys depart, "one little misunderstanding and them have to carry on like that?"

"Yeah," Christian sighed. "It almost makes me wish I never met Sharon. How I could know that big old Winston did like her? Him in the tenth grade! What him want with a ninth grader?"

"Probably the same thing you want with a ninth-grader," Robert grinned.

"Cho, man, be serious." Christian punched Robert on the shoulder. "She's just my friend and you know it."

As soon as Christian got home from school he threw his school bag onto the sofa and headed towards the back door. He knew his father would be out there tinkering with the old van that was parked under the sweetsop tree.

"Christian."

He stopped and turned towards the voice. "Yes, Ma," he groaned, not bothering to hide his annoyance.

"Christian," she called again, "come in here."

With a heavy sigh he dragged himself off to the kitchen. His mother stood at the kitchen sink, peeling green bananas.

As he approached she turned enquiring eyes to him. "Why are you home so late? Did you have club meeting today?"

"No, Ma." Christian flung himself onto the nearest chair. "I went to the library to do some research."

Princess dropped the knife into the pan of water and bananas and turned to him.

"You could have called."

"But I told you I have my project to work on."

"Yes, but you didn't mention that you were going to go to the library today." She dried her hands on a nearby towel. Her face became stern. "Christian, you know I'm not trying to be a grump but if it gets late and you're not home you know I'll worry. Just let me know where you are, okay?"

"Alright, Ma." Christian nodded then he sighed. "This assignment is so weird. I don't know where this teacher gets her ideas from."

"What's the assignment about?"

"Jamaican heritage but…but we have to make it different. The teacher said we could tie it to family or culture or music or something. I got some notes at the library but I don't know what to tie it to."

His mother began peeling more bananas but she looked thoughtful. "Jamaican heritage…sounds like fun."

"Yeah, right." Christian rolled his eyes at her.

"Just your cup of tea. You're such a bookworm." She grinned at him.

"I'm not." He frowned. He hated it when she called him that. It made him feel like a nerd.

She smiled and pulled out a chair from the kitchen table. She sat down beside him. "I like the idea of tying Jamaican heritage to our family. That would make your assignment even more interesting, don't you think?"

"I guess. But I don't want to talk about homework anymore, Ma. I'm going to go see Dad."

"Alright, just make sure both of you get inside in another half hour for dinner."

"Alright, Ma," Christian yelled as he dashed out the back door.

"Hey, Dad!"

Kevin Lee pulled his body from under the open bonnet at the sound of his son's greetings. He wiped greasy fingers on a rag already black with oil and nodded solemnly at his son. He was a serious man. His smiles were rare and he always seemed to have more than his fair share of problems on his mind.

But Christian loved his quiet, reserved father. He loved spending hours by his side tinkering with old cars, not saying much, just enjoying each other's company. Christian's father was the direct opposite of his mother, both in appearance as well as personality. Kevin Lee was dark, slim and small-bodied where she was big-boned and light-skinned. She was the talker in the family.

Christian was a miniature version of his father with his chocolate skin, slanted eyes, and wavy black hair. Sometimes he wished he looked more like his mother. At least then he would not be the brunt of jokes. The way he saw it if he were going to be teased for having Chinese blood then he should at least look Chinese. What was the point of having Chinese eyes with black skin?

What made it worse, the children at school assumed his family had money because of his Chinese name. Did all Chinese people own restaurants, wholesale outlets or supermarkets? His father was a mechanic.

"Ma said dinner will be ready in half an hour."

His father nodded again then turned and ducked his head under the open bonnet.

"What's wrong with it?

"Come." His father pulled out the dipstick. "Let me show you."

Christian awoke to the sound of a rooster crowing under his bedroom window. With a huge yawn he stretched and opened eyes still heavy with sleep. It was too dark to see clearly in the room so he closed his eyes again and snuggled further under the covers. The sun had just barely broken through the darkness so he knew it could not be later than five-thirty. As he lay enjoying the warmth of the blanket he heard his great-grandmother begin to stir in the next room. 'Why old people have to get up so early,' he thought, 'and the bed feel so sweet?'

Although she was in her eighties his great-grandmother never lay in bed until the sun was warm in the sky. The rooster's crow was her signal to start the day. The annoying thing was that by the time she threw open the windows and put the kettle on she would be pounding on his door. She held the firm belief that 'early to bed, early to rise' was the motto to live by. The way she followed it religiously you would think it was in the Bible.

Christian dug deeper under the toasty blankets and drifted into a comfortable doze.

"Christian. Chris, time for worship."

He groaned as the gravelly voice dragged him out of slumber. 'Geez,' he thought, 'why does she have to be so religious? It won't kill us to go one day without worship.' But he knew that if he did not stir within minutes she would come, bedroom slippers in hand, ready to slap him out of bed. With a groan he threw back the covers and reached for his robe.

Worship was thankfully brief this time so Christian was off to the yard shortly after six o'clock. The air was clear and countryside sweet and dew still covered the leaves and blades of grass. The smell of damp earth filled his nostrils and he took a deep, refreshing breath. His mother had sent him to spend part of the summer holidays with his great-grandmother so that he could do just that - breathe in some freshness and fill his lungs with unpolluted air.

Ever since he had turned twelve his asthma seemed to have gotten worse and his mother constantly blamed Kingston's polluted air. She said she had heard that smoke from the Riverton City Dump was causing respiratory illnesses in children in the Duhaney Park area. No matter that they lived all the way in Meadowbrook, the dump was to blame as far as she was concerned.

Every day she threatened to sue the government for Christian's illness. But she never tried. Instead, she took every opportunity to ship him off to the country to stay with his great-granny. She was even contemplating enrolling him in school there.

No way, he had objected. He would do it for the summer but there was no way he was going to live in that Saint Mary bush for good. Did she want him to end up talking like those country people? His mother had smiled when he had said that. She knew what he meant. She had often joked about country people's patois herself.

This visit to Granny's village was going to be different, though. He would be entering second form at the end of the holidays and all the students in his group had been instructed to work on a major project for presentation when they entered their new class.

Normally Christian did not even meet his new form teacher until the first day of school. Mrs. Preston had surprised the whole class when she showed up at their seventh grade class before the close of school in June and handed out assignment sheets. Of course, the general reaction had been a universal groan.

"Homework for the summer holidays? Cho!"

Strangely, Christian had been excited about the assignment: prepare a fifteen minute presentation on some aspect of Jamaican life, culture or heritage. They were supposed to research it during the summer holidays and have the presentation ready for the first week of school. He would be stuck in the country, anyway. The assignment would at least give him something to do on those long days.

When Granny Beth called him back into the house for breakfast he ran to wash his hands then sat down in front of a plate piled high with fried dumplings, fried plantains and Red Herring. A steaming mug of chocolate tea was beside the plate.

"Granny," he groaned, "you know I can't eat so much food."

"Eat up what I give you, boy! You don't see how you skinny? I want you to go back to Kingston with some flesh on your bones."

"But you skinny, too, Granny." Christian grinned at the old woman as she bent over him to place a dish of Otaheiti apples and guavas on the table. "How come you don't fatten up yourself?"

"Boy, the body get too old to fatten anymore. I just waiting on the Lord to call me home."

"Granny," Christian smiled, "you say that all the time."

"Hush and eat your food." She ruffled his wavy hair then turned back to the stove.

Christian dug into the food while he watched Granny at the sink as she washed the dishes. He took a sip of the hot tea then said, "Granny, can I…I mean, may I interview you today?"

"Interview me? Like one of them people on T.V.? What you goin' interview me 'bout?"

"About life in Bonny Gate, Granny, and about us."

"Us?"

"Yeah, you and me. Teacher said we must do a project on Jamaican heritage or history or something like that and I was just thinking I could do our family tree. That is like history, right?"

"You are absolutely right," she said. "You can learn a lot about a country by studying the people. And who better to study than your own family?" She sat down heavily in the chair beside him. "I only hope the old head can bear up to the strain of this work you giving me now. Is long time I don't work the old brain, you know."

"I know you can help me, Granny. You have to. I want to draw the family tree on cartridge paper and show it to the class for my presentation. Then I can tell everybody about the famous people who were in our family. We have some famous people, right, Granny?"

"Well, I don't rightly know 'bout famous but I know we have some God-fearing folks on our tree."

"God-fearing? It's famous people I want to talk about. We had any Prime Ministers? Or what about a prince? Or a pirate!"

"Lord, chile! Is where I goin' to find prince and pirate in the family?"

"But Granny, you have to, or else it won't be any fun," he pouted, "then I would have to think up a whole new idea for my project."

"Christian," Granny put her hand on his shoulder, "this is a serious project, right?"

When he nodded she continued, "Then you can't be looking for pirates and such the like. If you really want to know your roots then you have to accept the facts as they are."

Granny stared at him then, a knowing look in her eyes. "Christian Lee, I have a feeling there is more to this project than you telling me. I know you all your life and I know when you holding something back. You have that look on yuh face."

"Granny, is just a school project."

"I know…but why you pick a family tree to do?"

Christian looked embarrassed. Finally he said, "I want to know about me, Granny. I want to know why I look so weird."

"Weird? What you talking about, boy?"

His voice was little more than a whisper. "At school they call me 'mongrel'.

Granny drew in her breath sharply then hissed, "What! Why in the world…"

"Look at me, Granny." He cut her off. "My skin blacker than a lot of the children in my class but look how my hair stay. And look at my eyes!" He spat the words out as if they were a curse.

Granny Beth stared at Christian's tear-filled eyes then leaned over and gently pulled him into her arms.

"Christian, listen to me. Your grandfather on your father's side was Chinese. You know that. That's where you get your small eyes. And of course, your Mummy's father is an East Indian so that's why your hair is so wavy. With all them nation mix with African, you bound to look different. But what wrong with that?"

"But they laugh at me, Granny!"

"And you think a family tree going make them stop?"

"Well, if I show them how I come to look like this, maybe they won't bother me anymore."

"Christian, I know you young but you must have little more backbone that that, you know, pickney." Granny Beth was frowning now. "You are a handsome and intelligent boy so don't let anybody make you feel bad 'bout who you are. Your mother love you and give you all that she can afford and before your Grandma Leonie died, God rest her soul, she showed you the same love, if not more. You mus' listen to the people who love you, not them good-for-nutten idlers."

She straightened her back and folded her arms across her chest. "If you goin' to be a man worth him salt you have to be able to take a little ribbing sometimes and still stand up for yuhself. Anybody who call you names, jus' tell dem check you in ten years time and see who is the mongrel and who the pedigree."

Christian just sat there, still doubtful. Finally he sighed. "Yes, Granny, I hear you… but I still want to do the family history. You goin' help me?

"Of course, chile. What you want to know?"

"I want to know the first-first person in the family you can remember."

"Hmm, that is a hard one…but let me see if I can start at the very beginning. The first person, you say…" She paused and knitted her forehead in deep thought. After a moment, she spoke haltingly. "Well, I never rightly know this man…but my grandfather used to tell me about a rich, rich man that was him grandfather."

She paused again then continued slowly, "Him say that him never meet him because when him grandmother pregnant with him father she leave and go to some other parish. But him say she always tell him 'bout dis big straptin' white man, a plantation owner by the name of Adam Gordon…"

Chapter 9

2005

The sky was grey on the day of the funeral. The dusky shroud hung heavy overhead. There was no sun but the air was still and the heat dropped its dead weight on the village.

Gloria was dead. Beth's older sister had passed away in England. Before she died she had insisted on being laid to rest in the family plot in Bonny Gate. Her two older brothers were already gone so, of her mother's five children, only Beth and her younger brother Frederick were left.

The relationship between them was little more than nonexistent, with Frederick sending her a Christmas card at year-end and with her replying when she felt like it, or not at all.

Fred had done well in England where he had worked with the railroad. He owned two homes in Jamaica as well as another in Birmingham. He had three children who had all gone to university and five of his grandchildren had done the same. His youngest grandchild was studying neurosurgery on a full scholarship.

'Wonder if him would be so big and boasy if him did go through what me go through,' Beth thought as she yanked on the support stockings. 'Wonder if him would own a home in Kingston as well as Bonny Gate, plus send pickney to teachers college then to university? And what 'bout my business which thrive till me give it up when me turn seventy-five? How much of that him could do without the benefit of him fancy British education and a choicy job with the railroad?'

Now Fred was back in Jamaica at eighty-three years old, almost as stooped and withered as she was. In fact, she would say that she looked better than he did at her eighty-five years. One would think he was the one who had had a rough life. She snorted as she pulled on low-heeled black pumps. He did not know what rough life was.

Beth was trying to hurry as she got dressed but at her age dressing was a slow process. The arthritis made her clumsy. Her fingers fumbled on buttons and hooks that used to be so easy to latch.

She already had on her full slip and had stepped into her dress but the zipper was giving her a beast of a time.

"Princess. Princess!"

"Granny? You need something?" Princess called from the other room.

"Come here, me dear. Come help me with this zipper."

"Be there in a sec."

Beth flopped down in a chair by the window. She grabbed a magazine from a nearby table and began to fan her hot face. She hated to wear black so she had chosen this purple velvet dress but it made her so hot that she wondered if she could last through the whole funeral service with it on. She would definitely have to walk with her little battery-powered fan.

Princess entered the room, comb and brush in hand.

"What's up, Granny?"

Beth stood slowly then turned her back to the younger woman.

"See if you can pull up this zipper for me, nuh?" She shrugged her shoulders and tried to make herself smaller. "Look like I put on a little weight since the last time I wear it."

Princess smiled. "Granny, you've put on a lot of weight since the last time."

Beth nodded and smiled ruefully. "Is so it go when you get old. All manner of things happen to you. Now I goin' have to go on one of those crash diet that they promote on T.V."

As Princess pulled hard on the zipper she pulled her stomach in and tried to stand straighter. Gradually the zipper went up and Princess was able to close the hook at the top.

"Thank you, me chile," she sighed. She grabbed the magazine and began to fan again. "What a heat."

"But it's not that hot, Granny. There isn't even any sun outside."

"Ole people problem, me dear. The good Lord better hurry up and take me before anything else pile on top of mi troubles."

"Will you stop saying that? You're going to be around for many more years to come. Trust me." Princess grinned at her.

"The old man ready yet?"

When Princess looked at her quizzically Beth said, "Your granduncle."

"He's just putting on his tie right now. Everybody is just about ready so we can head out in another ten minutes."

She paused, then looking her grandmother in the eyes she asked, "Granny, why don't you ever call Uncle Fred by his name? You hardly even speak to him. It's as if you aren't related."

Beth was a little surprised by the question. "That's not true, dear. I talk to him. And I'm sure I call him by his name."

"No, you don't. And you get short-tempered with him, too."

"Where you get that from?"

"I see it every time you talk to him."

Beth thought for a moment then said, "Well, if you see me doing that it's not intentional. I didn't even realize it."

"Granny, just try to be nice today. Remember, both of you are saying goodbye to your older sister. Don't make it any harder than it has to be."

Beth stared hard at Princess then nodded. She turned to get her handbag.

The church was filled to capacity. Family alone filled the first eight pews. Beth sat in the front row sandwiched between Princess on the left and Fred on the right. She held the battery-powered fan right in front of her face. The heat was overwhelming.

Beth was sitting so close to the open casket that she could see the body of her dead sister lying there. The sickly sweet smell of embalming fluid assailed her nostrils and she covered her mouth and nose with a handkerchief as she fought a wave of nausea. She dug into her purse, fished out a mint and began to chew. The crowded church, the heat and the smell of death were all too much for her. She was dying for the service to be over.

She sneaked a glance at Fred who sat beside her, crumpling a piece of tissue in his large hands. He looked uncomfortable. She did not know if he just did not like funerals or if it was because it was his sister's funeral, but it was obvious to her that he did not want to be there. Well, neither did she. The choir began to sing and Beth tried to take her mind off her discomfort by humming along to their song.

"What a friend we have in Jesus, all our sins and griefs to bear, what a privilege to carry everything to God in prayer." As the last strains of the choir and the notes from the organ died away Beth dabbed at the beads of sweat settling on her upper lip.

The organist struck a chord and the entire congregation stood up. Surprised, Beth was slow in getting to her feet. Her arthritic knees were giving trouble again. As the organ music died away the Minister and his party entered and mounted the platform. Beth groaned. It was Pastor Philmore, one of the most long-winded preachers she knew. She was sure now that there was no hope of being released from this oven any time soon.

The congregation sat and Beth settled back into the seat. If they got up again for a song or a prayer she was just going to keep on sitting. Her knees could not take anymore. Pastor Philmore rose from his seat and approached the podium.

"My brethren," he said, "we are here to celebrate the life of a wonderful sister. She was the epitome of kindness, caring, sharing. We have lost a true sister with the death of this woman and she will be sorely missed."

As Beth listened she wondered how he knew all that. Gloria had lived in England for years. He did not know what she had been like. She was sure he was just saying all of that because it sounded good. Then, feeling ashamed of her wandering thoughts, she gave herself a mental shake and tried to concentrate on the sermon.

"Brothers and sisters, we have before us an angel of the Lord, a righteous and upright woman worthy of praise."

The amens rang out in the church.

"Now, brethren, it is for us to look into ourselves and determine whether we will be found worthy when the Lord calls us home." The pastor moved from behind the podium and began to pace the platform.

"Brethren, will we be found amongst the chosen? Will we walk the streets of gold? Will we have milk and honey and sit on the right hand of our Lord? Or…," he swung around and pointed to the congregation, "will we be roasted in the fires of hell?"

The hallelujahs were loud and someone at the back jumped up and screamed, "Jesus!"

"Are you worthy, brethren?" Pastor Philmore shouted as he pranced from one end of the platform to the other. "Have we been faithful with our tithes and offerings, brethren? Have we been giving back to the Lord his fair share of the fruits of our labour?"

Beth watched as the pastor bobbed and weaved, caught up in the emotion of his own sermon. He was like a crowing rooster gone mad. She raised the fan close to her face again. With Pastor Philmore's every hop she grew warmer. The more animated he became the more uncomfortable she became.

"Brothers and sisters, can we say at this moment, 'it is well, it is well with my soul'? Can we say, brethren, that if we are called home right now that we will walk hand in hand with our Lord and Saviour?"

With each question the organist struck a chord and the congregation shouted amens and hallelujahs. One woman on the choir waved her hands in the air, head bowed low, crooning "Jesus, Jesus". Another sprang to her feet with tears rolling down her face and cried, "Preach it, brother."

The pastor got louder and the congregation became more excited. There was a shriek from the back of the church and Sister Wilson dashed forward. She threw her plump body down at the altar.

"Yes, sister," the preacher cried, "throw your sins at the altar. Lay your burdens down before Jesus. If you are suffering, if you are worried, if the burden of sin is on your shoulders, lay them at the foot of the cross now. Come and wash in the blood of Christ and you will be whiter than snow."

Beth's head throbbed. The noise of the organ, the people screaming, the minister shouting – it was all too much. She dabbed feverishly at her brow then glanced at her brother. His forehead, too, was wet with perspiration. As she looked at him he returned the glance and gave her a weak smile.

She turned away quickly, annoyed. Why did he smile at her as if they had anything in common, she thought. There was nothing between them. They had only shared the same mother and father some long, long time ago. With a grunt she settled herself back into her seat and turned her eyes to the platform, determined never to look his way again.

It was almost seven o'clock before the family made it back to the house. The service had lasted almost two hours then they had spent another hour and a half at the family plot where the body was interred. By the time Beth was able to sit and put her feet up she was totally exhausted. She was too tired to even eat. The house was crowded with friends, family, church members, and children who were relieved to be free from the confines of the church. The little ones were now running around the house, screaming and getting on top of her nerves.

Beth escaped to her bedroom. She sat for a while in her favourite chair, just staring out the window and feeling the now cool breeze pass over her face. The fresh air soothed her. She leaned back and closed her eyes. For a long while she just sat there, listening to the soft sound of her own breathing, listening to the rustle of the wind in the trees. She was totally relaxed, drifting into sweet sleep, when there was a knock at the door.

"Who is it?" Beth's voice was soft and husky. She was still only half awake.

"Beth? It's Fred."

Beth blinked then stared at the closed door. For a while she did not answer. Then, in a stronger, sterner voice she said, "Yes? What is it?"

"May I come in?"

"I'm trying to get some rest," she replied curtly. "Is it something that can wait?"

"Beth." There was a pause then the voice came again. "Beth, you know I leave in the morning. I just wanted to talk to you."

Beth knitted her brow and grumbled to herself. She heaved a wearisome sigh. "Alright. The door is open. You can come in."

The door opened slowly. Fred pushed his white-haired head around it and peered in at her. He pushed the door open wider and entered then closed it behind him.

"Are you alright?"

"Yes. I jus' have a headache," Beth answered as she stared out the window, deliberately avoiding her brother's eyes. "I been trying to get away from the crowd and the noise but, as you can see, I was not too successful."

"I won't stay long," he said, sounding embarrassed. "It's just that, since I got here three days ago, I've been trying to get the chance to talk with you. But…you've always been so busy. Tonight is the last chance I will have to talk to you, Beth. I really don't want to go back home without us spending even a little while together."

Beth turned to stare at him but said nothing. Fred fiddled with his tie then looked away. He sidled over to a small bench by the bedside and perched on the edge. He looked like a little boy who had done something wrong and was asking his mother for forgiveness. It was obvious that he was not comfortable with her silence. Beth did nothing to make it easier for him. She just sat there looking at him.

"Beth, I know we are not very close because you grew up for most of your teenage years in Kingston and I was in the country. Then I was sent off to England. We are old people now in our eighties and I know it is late for us to even want to be close, but I just want to try." He pulled on the tie again. "The two of us are the only ones left and for whatever little time we have here on earth I would really like us to keep in touch."

"What you want me to do?" Beth looked at him, frowning. "From the time I was fourteen I was forced out of the family. And you want me to be a part of it now? Now, when everybody dead and it's just the two of us left?"

"Beth, you were always a part of the family. You know that. And that is why we always kept trying to make contact with you. I wrote to you many times from England but you never replied. And even Gloria tried to contact you once she started working. But it's as if you always tried to push us away. You were the one rejecting us."

"Me? That's a laugh. I wanted to be part of the family but yet I was the one who was sent away to Kingston. Given away! I was the one who had to suffer at the hands of men trying to maul me. I was the one who had to survive on my own without the help of mother or father while the four of you lived happily with them." Beth glared at him. "You and Gloria had the privilege of going to England. Simon went to the States and Albert did very well for himself before he died. But me, I had to struggle through everything - alone. Where were you all when I needed my family?"

Fred looked shocked at the vehemence with which she spoke. "Beth, you know that the only reason mother sent you away was because we were so poor. She knew she couldn't manage and she thought there was more opportunity for you in Kingston. She never wanted to lose contact with you once you were there."

He came a little closer to her, speaking earnestly. "She loved you and she tried her best to get you back but every time she tried to get in touch with you, you refused to reply to her letters. You made it seem as if you were managing great all on your own. It was not until you were a big woman with a child that you even started speaking to Mama again."

"And what you expect? I know she hated me. She found it so easy to get rid of me. Why did she have to give me away?" Beth shook her head angrily, feeling the tears well up inside her. With all her might she fought the rush of emotions, fought to hold on to the shell that protected her heart.

But it was no use. She had hid behind her tough façade for years but now the tears were coming, washing away the hardness that covered her soft core. She buried her face in her hands. She sat there for a long time, her body shaking, her breath catching on heaving sobs she was struggling to control.

When she looked up again her wrinkled face was wet with the tears of her childhood pain. "I was always the outsider, never a part of the Gordon family. Sometimes I didn't know who I really was. I even wondered if they had adopted me and then just got fed up and wanted to get rid of me. I know people who were poor, just as poor as we were, and they held on to their children. They tried their best and they never let go. So why did Mama have to let me go?"

Fred got up from the stool and walked over to Beth. He reached out a trembling hand and touched her arm. "I know you're hurt. I know the family hurt you more than we ever realized. We tried to be in touch with you, to bring you back into the family and you refused our efforts. But we should never have stopped trying."

He stepped back and turned his face away from her. He pulled a handkerchief from his pocket and pressed it to his left eye and then the right. "We just thought…we just thought everything was fine with you because that is what you kept saying. You never let on that you were suffering, that you were in pain, that you even wanted us as your family. You were always so independent…probably too independent for your own good."

He shook his head as if to get rid of the bad memories. Then he looked at her. "Beth, please know that we all loved you. And I…I'm here and I still love you."

Beth looked up at him and her old heart ached. She ached for this brother she had once loved, she yearned for the family she had once had. Still, she remained silent. There was nothing she could say. It was all too late.

Fred watched his sister's face. He, too, remained silent. Then slowly, hesitantly, he took her hand. He sat on the edge of the bed, still holding on to her.

"Sis, I have something to tell you." There was a look of sorrow on his face. "Something that might make you understand."

Beth looked back at him and felt her heart pound in her chest. "What is it?" she whispered.

"This is something I promised I would never tell. But in all fairness to you, I think I must."

"What you talkin' about?" She squeezed his hand, wishing he would just speak up. Her poor heart could not take much more this day.

"I promised Gloria that I would take this to my grave but there is something I have to tell you…about our parents."

The distress was evident on his face. Beth held her breath and waited, all the while thinking, my heart, my poor heart can't take any more pain.

Fred freed his hand from her grip and got up. He began to pace the room.

"Sister Gloria told me that, as the oldest girl, she used to get all the attention of our father. He called her…his 'Princess'.

Beth exhaled slowly and looked away. She looked out the window at the green hills and the banana tree swaying in the evening breeze. She felt the hurt seeping into her bones. "His princess? But…I used to be Papa's princess."

"Yes, but Gloria was his princess first. He told her that she was his special girl. She used to do special things for him."

"Just like I used to do?"

"I don't know. Maybe." Now Fred sounded wary, confused.

"He used to let me be responsible for shining his shoes and putting out his clothes for church." Beth smiled sadly. She felt a warm rush of love as she remembered her beloved Papa.

"Gloria used to do that, too." Fred nodded. "But…there's more."

"Yes?" Tears were beginning to fill her eyes again.

"Our father…," Fred screwed up his eyes and put a shaking hand to his head. "Our father used to molest Gloria."

"M…molest? You mad?" The pounding in her chest was back, louder, frightening her. "How could you say these things about Papa?"

"Beth, I'm sorry. It's all true." The crumpled white handkerchief appeared again and Fred dabbed at his eyes. He blew his nose and drew in a shaky breath. Then he continued. "He used to do things with her that were not right, Beth. He called her his special princess and he would make her do things…you know what I mean."

"Oh, my God," Beth whispered. She clutched the front of her blouse, pressing her fist hard against her chest, against her heart. Of all the people in her family, her father was the only one she had kept on loving, kept on hoping would come for her. She had never stopped loving him. And now this! My heart, she thought, my poor heart is too old for this. Too old.

"Are you sure?" she whispered. When Fred nodded she said. "But why? Why would he do that? Gloria loved him so much. And…and so did I."

"Yes, I know. And Mama knew that too. When she found out what was going on she immediately shipped you off to Kingston because she did not want that to happen to you, too. She heard him starting to call you his princess and she realized what was going to happen to you."

"Is that why he left the house soon after I did? I knew when he left. I heard about it at the market, from the country people."

"Yes, that's right. Mama told him he had to leave the house or else she would report everything to the police and he would be locked away for good."

"So it was not because of money that she sent me away or…because she did not like me." Beth's voice trailed off.

"Well, money had something to do with it but it was more the situation with Papa. She wanted you to be safe. Later on, when she was able to manage a little bit better she wanted you to come back home but you refused. That time you were about seventeen and you said you had a nice job in Kingston and you weren't interested in coming back home. Eventually she gave up."

Beth did not respond. She just sat there, trying to absorb the shocking news. The father she had revered had been a devil all along.

"You know, it was really hard on her when Papa left," Fred continued. His voice was low and sad but his tears were gone. "That is why she gave me away to Pastor Simpson. He sent me to one of his cousins in England. It's the same cousin who sent for Gloria. They let us work in the house and we were able to go to school in the evenings. That is how we survived."

"She gave you away, too?"

"Yes, she did. She had to. She was all alone and it was hard for her."

"So why didn't Gloria tell me what was going on?"

"She knew how much you loved Papa, and Mama knew too. They were so ashamed. They were afraid to tell you what he was really like. I think he was sick."

Beth sighed deeply. Her heart had slowed to a steady pounding and her hands were steady in her lap. "So all those years when I thought you all didn't want me in the family and I kept avoiding all of you, I was wrong."

"Well, you were wrong about why you were sent away, and you were wrong in thinking that we did not love you. But we were wrong, too. We should never have taken your statements at face value. Even if you were doing well, even if you said you did not need us anymore and your life was great, we should have insisted on being a part of your life. We should have tried to be there for you. I guess we were just taking the easy way out."

As Beth heard her brother speak she could feel the remnants of her exterior shell crumble. She had always put on this strong, determined front in front of everyone but deep down inside she had been crying for the love she felt no one had ever given her. She desperately wanted to be loved.

"All this time I have been resenting my mother and all this time she really loved me," she said softly. "I thought she was jealous of me because Papa loved me and called me his princess. But she was just protecting me and I didn't even know it." She bit her lower lip. "I drove you all away with my stubbornness."

Fred put his arm around her. "Don't blame yourself, Beth. You were innocent in all of this. You didn't know what was going on."

"I didn't know, but I could have given her a chance. I could have given all of you a chance. I was so stubborn." She rested her hand on Fred's arm and looked up at him, wondering if he would ever understand. "All that time I stayed away, rejected the family it was because… I felt I didn't belong. Sometimes I didn't even know who I was."

"Beth," Fred whispered, and bent low to squeeze her tight to him, "with all your stubbornness I know who you are. You're a Gordon, through and through."

With tears running down their faces brother and sister hugged each other close and cried.

Epilogue

At the time of her birth the island had been gentle and kind. At the present time she is far from that. In recent years Jamaica has had one of the highest murder rates in the world, jockeying with countries like South Africa and Brazil for the top spot. In the years following Independence she has been plagued with economic recession, high inflation and currency devaluation. She sheds tears daily for the children she has lost to the AIDS epidemic.

Jamaica has had more than her fair share of trials. However, like Beth, this woman has weathered the storms of life. Through it all she is still smiling, still achieving, still growing.

Even as she cries for her children she has room in her heart to welcome the children of others. Jamaica's tourism product attracts visitors from far and wide and as the industry has developed so her people have progressed. 2006 data indicates positive trends in inflation (down to 6%), unemployment (down to 8.9%) and nominal GDP (2.9% growth). Her people are educated (88%) and are communicating – among themselves and with the world – with mobile telephone penetration of 95%...and growing.

This woman, so petite and yet so powerful, has influenced the world in so many ways. She has been a leader in music. 1970's Dancehall Reggae was the starting point for the now celebrated African American Hip-Hop music, also known as Rap Music. The music form has two components: rapping (MCing) and DJing (production and scratching). DJ Kool Herc (Clive Campbell from Kingston, Jamaica who emigrated to the Bronx, NY) is the originator of this Hip-Hop/ Rap form. He started out with his sound system, "toasting" to the music of Jamaican reggae artistes such as U-Roy and I-Roy. He later used funk records because of the growing demand for his toasting. Later, the relationship between Dancehall and Hip-Hop was renewed with the music of Yellow Man, KRS-One and Shabba Ranks. Today, Sean Paul and Shaggy continue the legacy. The relationship between Jamaican Dancehall and Hip-Hop remains strong.

Her son, Bob Marley, continues to dominate the music world decades after his death. Time Magazine voted his album, *Exodus*, the most important album of the twentieth century. His anthem, *One Love*, was designated Song of the Century by the BBC. This 'dreadlocks Rastaman' brought the plight of the Third World to all nations through his philosophy, his lyrics and his refusal to be dominated by 'Babylon'.

Coming out of this musical heritage is Jamaica's love for dance which has been so infectious that some of her moves have been adopted into the dances of other nations. Looking back at Rap/Hip-Hop culture, Clive Campbell's influence did not only reach the music but dances were created as well: Break-dancing is still popular in the urban American community and can be seen in countries as far away as Slovenia. Dances created by

Jamaican locals, such as the Butterfly and the Bogle, are sometimes seen in American music videos.

Jamaica's Dancehall culture has also led us into the risqué world of Dancehall fashion. One only needs to watch a few of the popular music videos to observe some of these fashions on display. For its part the Reggae culture, with Bob Marley at the helm, has influenced the hair style of many persons of various nations, with many people of black, white and even Asian heritage now choosing to wear their hair in dreadlocks.

In the field of athletics there is no denying that Jamaica is a world leader. Her reputation as the "sprint factory" is cast in stone. She is the mother of famous Olympic champions such as Donald Quarrie, Merlene Ottey, Deon Hemmings and Aleen Bailey. Even those who were adopted by others remember Jamaica as their mother: Donovan Bailey and Ben Johnson of Canada, and Lynford Christie of Great Britain. Her young son, Asafa Powell, is the 2006 World Athlete of the Year. Not to be forgotten is her first Bobsled team which competed in the Winter Olympics in Calgary, Canada in 1988. They competed with determination despite their handicap of having to train on the sandy beaches rather than in snow.

Jamaica has also made her mark in the political arena. Jamaican national hero, Marcus Mosiah Garvey, was the founder of the United Negro Improvement Association, the first important black nationalist movement in America and the largest African American organization in that country's history. He sought to end imperialist rule, and to encourage travel and trade between black businesses in the USA and Africa through the shipping company, Black Star Line. More importantly, though, this son of her loins taught Black people around the world to have pride in their heritage, and was one of the earliest catalysts for the American Civil Rights Movement. Marcus Garvey was one of the most influential black leaders of the twentieth century.

On top of all this, our lady is a great cook. Her jerk seasoning, an inheritance from the Tainos, is known around the world. Her beef patty, hard dough bread and spiced bun can be had in numerous countries and her rice and peas and curried goat have graced many a sophisticated table. Her cuisine is a fitting representation of her motto, "Out of many, one people".

In short, this woman – Jamaica, land we love - she little, but she "tallawa".

And her story continues…

Source: Wikipedia - The Free Encyclopedia < http://en.wikipedia.org>

About the Author

Judy Powell is a Jamaican Writer and Marketing Consultant living in Ontario, Canada. She has lived and worked in various countries including France, Puerto Rico, the USA and Canada. She has also travelled extensively in the Caribbean and Latin America. In addition to English she speaks Spanish, French, and a smattering of German.

Judy holds a Bachelor of Arts in Foreign Languages/ International Business Administration as well as a Master of Arts in Spanish and an M.B.A. in Marketing. She is working on a third Master's Degree in Humanities/ Literature. She is a member of the U.S.A. Honour Society, Phi Beta Kappa.

Judy enjoys hearing from her readers. Please feel free to contact her through her website at www.judypowell.com or by e-mail: info@judypowell.com